Crooked River
Shelley Pearsall

Alfred A. Knopf
NEW YORK

THIS IS A BORZOI BOOK PUBLISHED BY ALFRED A. KNOPF

Text copyright © 2005 by Shelley Pearsall
Jacket design copyright © 2005 by Alfred A. Knopf
All rights reserved under International and Pan-American Copyright Conventions.
Published in the United States of America by Alfred A. Knopf, an imprint of Random
House Children's Books, a division of Random House, Inc., New York, and simultaneously
in Canada by Random House of Canada Limited, Toronto. Distributed by
Random House, Inc., New York.

KNOPF, BORZOI BOOKS, and the colophon are registered trademarks of Random House, Inc.

www.randomhouse.com/kids

Library of Congress Cataloging-in-Publication Data
Pearsall, Shelley.
Crooked river / Shelley Pearsall. — 1st ed.
p. cm.
SUMMARY: When thirteen-year-old Rebecca Carver's father brings a Native American
accused of murder into their 1812 Ohio settlement town, Rebecca, witnessing the town's
reaction to the Indian, struggles with the idea that an innocent man may be convicted
and sentenced to death.
ISBN 0-375-82389-1 (trade) — ISBN 0-375-92389-6 (lib. bdg.)
1. Ojibwa Indians—Juvenile fiction. [1. Ojibwa Indians—Fiction. 2. Indians of North
America—Ohio—Fiction. 3. Family life—Ohio—Fiction. 4. Frontier and pioneer life—
Ohio—Fiction. 5. Ohio—History—19th century—Fiction. 6. Trials (Murder)—Fiction.]
I. Title.
PZ7.P3166Cr 2005
[Fic]—dc22
2004010310

Printed in the United States of America
August 2005
10 9 8 7 6 5 4 3 2 1
First Edition

For Mike

The two principles on which our conduct towards the Indians should be founded are justice and fear.

—Thomas Jefferson, 1786

April 1812

it is the time when the leaves
are small on the trees.
too small
for hiding.

the gichi-mookomaanag—
white men—
hunt for us.

run, i whisper to Little Otter.
run like a fast-melting spring river.
do not look back.
run.

he is quick,
Little Otter,
and slips like a soft fish
through their hands.

but Ten Claws and i
are not so lucky.

one snap
of the white man's gun
and he is dead.
i am caught.

One

Pa never told us he would capture an Indian and bring him back across the river. Never breathed a word that he would march an Indian right into our cabin and make him a prisoner while we were gone away. Only thing he told us was that he was going across the Crooked River to see about a few savages who were causing trouble.

Now, if our poor Ma had been alive, I don't expect he would have ever dared to do such a shameful thing. Not if she had been standing in the doorway with her Bible clutched to her chest, he wouldn't have. But Ma was gone, and me and my sister Laura had set out in pouring rain to help the Hawleys, who had all taken sick with a fever.

The Hawleys lived up the road from us, where it was mostly uncleared woods. And truth to speak, they were the kind who were always falling sick, or getting bit by a snake, or being thrown off their miserable horse. Never should have come out to the Ohio frontier in the first place, Pa often said.

We had been on the frontier for nearly twelve years, so we were as seasoned as salt. The Evans family, who lived in the opposite direction from the Hawleys, had come from Vermont not long after us. Right past the Evanses' log house was old Vinegar Bigger's cabin—he was as old as the saints, folks said.

And if you kept on going, past Mr. Bigger's cabin, past the woods where the pigeons were fond of roosting, past the muddiest part of the road, past a thicket of greenbriers on your left, you would reach the small settlement on the Crooked River. It had about fifty more people who, in late summer, were often as sick as the Hawleys on account of the fevers caused by the swampy river.

"You coming, Laura?" I hollered as we made our way toward the Hawleys' cabin. I pushed back the hood of my cloak to look for my sister, who was lagging somewhere behind me in the rain.

Laura was seventeen, four years older than me, and she had always been big for a girl. No matter how much our Ma had added and mended, Laura's clothes kept up a never-ending tug-of-war around her body, and her dresses were always too short to cover up her thick ankles and wide white feet. Pa called her "our horse." That's what he said when folks came to visit.

"This here's Laura. Our big horse," he'd laugh, in

that loud way of his. "Gonna have to turn her out to pasture if she keeps on growing like she is."

Then he'd nod at me. "And this here's Rebecca," he'd say. "She looks like her Ma did, but she's slow in the head, and lazy, and don't do a quarter of the work."

I was not slow in the head. Or lazy.

But we would just keep our heads down and not say a word whenever Pa was talking to folks. No matter what he called us.

Since our Ma had died, me and Laura had only ourselves for company. Our three-year-old sister, Mercy, was nothing but a babbling pester. And our two brothers, Amos and Lorenzo, along with our miserable cousin George, who lived in our cabin, had no use for us except for the three meals we set in front of them every day.

Breakfast, noonday dinner, and supper. That's all we were to them.

Sometimes after the supper meal was through, me and Laura would set by the hearth, and if she wasn't too awful tired, Laura would brush the bird nests out of my brown hair, same as Ma had once done. And often, I did Laura's mending in the evenings because my fingers were small and quick. And my eyesight was good, where hers wasn't. So that's the way we filled in some of what was missing without Ma.

As me and Laura drew closer to the Hawleys' log house, I noticed there wasn't a whisper of smoke coming from their chimney, a bad sign, surely. "No fire going," I pointed.

Laura tugged her wet cloak tighter around her shoulders. "Well, we are just gonna knock on that door and see what we find," she said, casting a jumpy look at the cabin and taking a deep breath.

Turned out, poor Mrs. Hawley was nearer to death than life. I reckon it was a good thing we had come when we did because she couldn't even stir from her bed to fetch a cup of water or a crust of bread for her ailing husband and children. And the smell in that place could have nearly kilt you.

Laura sent me back to our house to fetch some hot coals to start a fire, and she said I should gather up a full basket of food for the Hawleys. Even though it was still pouring rain, I ran part of the way back just to get the smell of the Hawleys' place out of my head.

My brother Lorenzo was sitting inside our cabin when I returned. He had been left to keep an eye on little Mercy, but he had himself pulled up to a big platter on the table, and he was picking out the left-over pieces of cold pork from breakfast with his fingers instead. Pick. Chew. Pick. Chew.

One of the fresh loaves that me and Laura had baked the day before was sitting on the table with its end crumbled in where he had tunneled through it with his fingers.

I glared at him. "We was saving that bread for supper."

Lorenzo was eleven, two years younger than me, and he was named after my Pa, so that showed you something right there. He could do whatever he pleased. Always acted like he was the biggest toad in the puddle. Always grabbed the biggest piece of meat from the supper table and took the warmest part of the hearth for his seat.

"No one told me a thing, and I was hungry," he said, sticking his greasy fingers back into the pile of pork again. Pick. Chew.

Nobody vexed me as much as Lorenzo.

I pushed the basket onto the table. "Make your lazy old self useful and help git some things together for the Hawleys. They've all got the fever bad."

"Ain't that a pity." He grinned. "Poor Hawleys."

Anger pinched my throat and squeezed my ribs. *Poor Hawleys.* Reaching out, I dug my fingers as hard as a horse's teeth into his left arm, trying to make him mind me. Who was gonna make him listen if me and Laura didn't? "You go on and git a string of beans from the loft so we can make a soup for the Hawleys."

Lorenzo yanked his arm away. "Can't," he said. "There's a murderous savage up there, and I ain't about to set one foot in the loft. But you can go on up if you've a mind to." Lorenzo gave me one of his half-crooked grins and brushed a lock of brown hair out of his eyes.

Now I didn't know a thing about the Indian right then. Not one thing. I figured Lorenzo was just spinning another miserable lie to get himself out of doing any decent work, same as he always did. I remember hollering at him, "I'm so awful sick of your stories—I'll go up to the loft myself and look for your killer Indian just to prove what a lazy yarn spinner you are."

Snatching the basket off the table, I started up the narrow stairs furiously, not even taking care to watch the edge of my dress. It would serve Lorenzo right if my feet got tangled in my skirts and I fell down the steps, cracked my head on the plank floor, and died.

Below me, I could hear the sound of Lorenzo's chair scraping back from the table. "You best take care," he called out.

Although I went up to the chamber loft nearly every day to fetch something, I never took much of a liking to it. The long, low-ceilinged room had only two small windows, one at each end, and you could hear mice rustling about in the shadows. Each time I reached my hand into an apple barrel or cut down a string of beans up there, I was tormented by the thought that one of those mice would go skittering up my arm.

"Lorenzo, this Indian of yours surely better be something to look at," I said loudly as Lorenzo stood by the foot of the stairs. I squinted into the shadows of the loft, figuring that Lorenzo had hung an old coat from one of the rafters. Or fixed up a hat with goose feathers. That would be just the sort of thing he would do.

But I was wrong.

There in the loft, not more than a few steps away, was a real Indian staring straight back at me. My heart just about flew out of my chest at the sight, and I screamed.

Two

I'm real ashamed to say that after seeing that Indian, I bolted from the cabin and tore down the road in the rain. Likely looked as if I had gone and caught myself on fire as I ran toward the settlement with my petticoats and bonnet strings flying.

I was so full of petrification, I never stopped for a minute to think why the Indian might be sitting there and what all Lorenzo knew.

And then I did the second wrong thing.

I yelled for help.

"Indians!" I shouted, and belted out every name I knew—Pa, Amos, Laura, the Hawleys, even Ma, who was gone, and Grandpa Carver back in the East. It was as if demons had taken possession of my voice and it was just shrieking out names on its own. I couldn't stop it.

All of the men within earshot came running at the dreadful sound of it. My older brother, Amos, came tearing across the field where he had been fixing a fence. Mr. Evans and old Vinegar Bigger flew out of their houses to help me. Even my Pa appeared, slopping down the muddy road with his rifle in his hand and a half dozen men from the settlement behind him. And that stopped me in my tracks.

My Pa.

I stood there in the middle of the road with my teeth rattling away on their own, trying to make sense of what I was seeing and all of the questions they were hollering at me. "You hurt? Were they Chippewas? How many? Which direction'd they go? Where's Lorenzo? Did they carry him off? Speak up, girl—"

That last voice was my Pa's.

"I says speak up," he roared, moving close enough to strike me if he had a reason to. "Stop standing there like the village idiot and shaming your Pa. You tell the men exactly what you seen."

Everyone got real quiet after that. The only sound was the rain splattering on the leaves around us. The men's eyes looked down at the ground because they all knew about my Pa. He had a temper like a timber rattlesnake, and even grown men kept their distance when they saw his anger rising. Everyone called him Major Carver. But my Pa wasn't the major of any army of soldiers—just gave orders to our settlement and us Carvers. And that was miserable enough.

"I seen an Indian, Pa," I whispered, trying to keep

my voice from shattering to pieces. "There's an Indian hiding up in our loft."

Pa's eyes narrowed. "One Indian?" he said sharply. "That all you saw? One Indian?"

I nodded. "Yes sir."

At this, one of the men gave a big snort of laughter and some of the other men started to chuckle and exchange glances among themselves, as if they all knew something I didn't. I watched them rest the ends of their rifles on the ground as if they didn't mind one bit what I'd told them about Indians. Even my serious brother Amos shook his head and broke into a little smile. I could feel a red flush creep into my face as I stood there with all of the men laughing at me.

"I ain't lying," I hollered in a voice that was choking up fast with tears. "You go on back there and see. I ain't lying." I waved my arms in the direction of the house.

But the men just kept on chuckling and rolling their eyes at every word I said. Vinegar Bigger, who was standing near me, patted my shoulder with his old hand. He leaned over and said in a loud whisper, "Course you ain't lying, girl. We know there's an Indian in your Pa's house, 'cause we the ones who put him there."

We the ones who put him there.

This was the first I realized what my Pa and the men had done. I imagine that my face went as white as a wall right then. All I knew was that the men had gone across the Crooked River to see about a few Indians who were causing trouble. They hadn't breathed a word about what kind of trouble or why. And now they wanted me to understand that they had brought back one of those savages and put him in our own house?

I didn't understand a thing.

"Go on." My Pa gestured to the men. "Go on back to what you was doing. Sorry she brought you running. Real sorry for your trouble."

My Pa waited until the men were gone to start laying out all of his worst words on me. After they left, his face went straight from being soft with laughter to hard with meanness. "I don't know what the devil got into you, Rebecca," he swore. "Running and screaming for help like you was being scalpt—that ain't funny at all, you understand me?" His voice got louder. "You understand me? You made us Carvers look like a bunch of fools." He spat out each word. Bunch. Of. Fools.

"Look at me!" Pa's voice roared.

My heart thudded in my chest, fearing what he might do. His hand grabbed hold of my face, and his rough fingers dug into my cheeks. "I won't stand to look like a fool," he spat. "You ever do something like that again, I'll take a razor strop to you. You understand me?"

I nodded.

His fingers squeezed harder. "I'm your Pa. You answer me with a 'yes sir.'" He leaned over and hollered in my face, so close I could smell the sour tobacco on his breath. My Pa's teeth were stained brown, and the corners of his mouth were yellowed like paper before it catches fire and burns.

"Yes sir," I whispered.

"You ain't fit for the grease pot, you know that? You make me ashamed to have you as a daughter." He swore and gave me a hard push. "Git back to the house."

All the way through the woods, with the rain falling in buckets around me, I thought about how I purely hated my Pa.

Three

My brother Amos was waiting for me when I got back. Most times, he had a softer heart than my Pa and the others. He was nearly twenty, with my Pa's dark hair but my Ma's light-colored eyes. Every once in a while, Ma's eyes had given me the smallest flicker of kindness when they weren't filled up with worry or weariness. And Amos was the same way. If I looked up fast enough, there were times I caught something like Ma's kind look in his eyes.

"Seeing that Indian was a considerable surprise, I expect," Amos said before I'd even closed the door. I gave a quick squint-look around. Our log house was big, but it was all one room. Except for the loft, you could see it in a single glance—the beds, the hearth, everything. There was no sign of Lorenzo. Just Amos sitting by himself, with his wide plow shoulders hunched over our big dinner table.

"Yes," I said low. "It was."

"But that didn't give you no cause to run, Reb," he continued. "You coulda got somebody kilt, the way you were hollering about Indians chasing you when there weren't none."

I dug my fingernails into my palms. Last thing I wanted to hear from Amos was an echo of my Pa. I was always getting the blame for everything gone wrong. Slow in the head. Lazy. Not fit for the grease pot.

"I didn't mean to scare nobody," I said, louder.

Amos kept his eyes on the table and picked up crumbs with the end of his finger. "Well, maybe Pa shoulda told you that he was bringing the Indian here, but that still didn't give you no cause to act like you did." Amos frowned and shook his head. "You gotta turn the current of your mind to do more thinking, Reb. You are like a buzzing little fly that don't ever think. You just go headfirst right into things."

I was not a buzzing little fly.

Both of us were silent for a while, with the rain drumming on the roof, Amos picking up more crumbs, and me not moving from where I stood as my cloak dripped water all over the floor.

Finally, Amos sighed loudly and said, "I don't mind telling you why the Indian's here, but you gotta promise you won't fall into a fit over this, Reb, or go running out of the house screaming for Pa and the men."

Inside my mind, I thought that if the house caught fire right then, a windstorm was toppling all of the trees in the woods, and Indians were attacking—nothing, absolutely nothing, would make me run.

But I didn't say that to Amos. I just nodded and told him I would never do a fool-headed thing like that again. Ever. "Fine," Amos said, leaning back in his chair. "Then I'll tell you what Pa and the other men have done."

for two days
the rain falls
in long drops
from the clouds.

for two days
the gichi-mookomaanag
pull me
through the weeping woods
and across
the crooked running river.

i am tied to a long iron rope.
i do not come easily.

when we reach the log house
of the tall man
with the black hair of the bear
and the eyes of the snake,
i am placed
in a room that floats
above the ground.

in the room
where the tall man keeps
his winter food,
i am stored
like a sack of parched corn
or a bag of wild rice.

you will die soon,
the gichi-mookomaanag
say to me.

Windigo,
the flesh-eating giant,
will devour you
by the next moon,
i tell them.

and they
do not understand
a word.

Four

Amos told me that the men had gone across the Crooked River to find three Indians who had kilt a white trapper named Gibbs and stole all his traps. One of the three Indians was real young. But Amos said the young one got away and the second one, an older Indian, kilt himself with a gun. So, they brought back just one.

According to Amos, it took the men two days in the pouring rain to drag the Indian back to the settlement, and they had to pull him the whole way at the end of a chain. The savage Indian was known by the name Indian John, and the men were gonna put him on trial for murder and hang him.

Now, my Pa had done a lot of terrible things in his life. I could name more than a few of them. He had beat a fellow within an inch of his life. Shot a neighbor's dog for drinking a pan of milk in our springhouse. Thrown a chair once at our poor Ma.

But nothing as dreadful bad as putting a murderer in our own house, above our own heads.

Amos insisted that there wasn't any other place. "Can't have some savage running loose in the woods, killing other poor folks. You want that, Reb?" Amos had said. "He's just gonna stay here until the trial. Pa's got him in leg irons and chains. Ain't gonna hurt no one."

It was true that our settlement on the Crooked River didn't have a jail yet. It had one narrow mud road called Water Street, which ended at the river. About two dozen cabins and dwellings—some still unfinished—were scattered along the road. In between, there were three small taverns for travelers and two pitiful, half-empty stores where you could buy Bateman's drops, and salt, and not much else. But, even though our settlement didn't have a proper jail, I still didn't think my Pa had the right to use our cabin as one.

Lying in bed that night, me and Laura couldn't even close our eyes for fear that the Indian would slip down from the chamber loft and murder us in our sleep. The bedstead that was Laura's and mine stood closest to the stairs.

"What are we gonna do?" I whispered to Laura, my voice rising in the darkness. "If he comes down those steps, what will we do?"

Mercy slept on a straw pallet set on the floor beside us. Pa and the boys were on the other side of the old quilt that hung between our beds. I could already hear Pa's rattling snore.

Laura whispered that she didn't care what Pa said, she was going to fetch the knives from the shelf by the hearth and we would put them between the ropes that held our bed. So, that's what we did. I had the sharp knife that we always used for paring apples, and Laura had our biggest butchering knife.

But I wasn't sure if putting the knives beneath our bed made me feel more or less terrified at the place we were in. Or if we would ever be able to curl our fingers around the handles and use them. And what if the Indian crept down the stairs before we heard him? Or a whole band of Indians attacked us from the outside? What would we do then?

The darkness outside the house was filled with the echoing sounds of early spring frogs. They were loud that night, making a noise like a thousand jangling harness bells, and I knew we would never hear the soft sounds of approaching Indians.

Lying there, I couldn't keep my mind from twisting and turning on its own. Thinking about all the stories I'd heard of what Indians had done. Pa and the trappers who came through would tell these kinds of stories in low voices, leaving out more words than they kept in. "A whole family. Four children. And an old woman. Seventy years old. A crying shame. Right in their beds while they slept. Near Black Fork. Burnt to the ground."

What if we were kilt by Indians—what would happen then? Would me and Laura open our eyes and find ourselves in the eternalized world? Would

Ma suddenly appear next to our bed, wearing her faded green dress, and lead us away? Thinking about it made my whole body turn cold as pond ice. I surely wanted to be saved from the evil to come—and to see our dear Ma again—but I didn't feel ready to die. Not right then, I didn't.

Ma had always been fearful of Indians. "They are the work of the devil," she would tell Pa or anyone else who brought up the subject. "No different than rattlesnakes, catamounts, or wolves. Nothing but savage beasts in human skin."

Savage beasts in human skin.

I slid my fingers carefully along the bed ropes, searching for the knife again, making certain it was where I remembered. My throat tightened as my fingers suddenly touched the smooth wooden handle, and I felt as if I would be sick. I wanted to take it back to the hearth. That was the honest truth. I didn't want to keep it under my bed. Nor kill anybody with it. Not even a savage Indian.

in the night
i listen,
i walk through the darkness
with my ears.

seven voices sleep below—
the tall man
with the black hair of the bear,
and six other ones.

they do not sleep softly.

the tall man snores through his nose
and rumbles
and groans.
a small one is fitful and cries out,
and two girls whisper together
like leaves,
sh-sh-sh-sh.

i close my eyes
and think
of my wife Rice Bird,
and the two Old Ones
who live in our bark lodge,
and my brave son
Little Otter,
and quiet Yellow Wing,
only four winters old,

who does not make a sound
when she sleeps.

i walk through the other lodges
in our half circle
and I think about the men
who will not come
for me.

my father is old,
Small Hawk and Half Sky
are gone to war,
Ten Claws is dead.

in the darkness,
the five lodges of our small band
are silent
and empty of men.

Five

When the morning birds started up singing and the light in the room turned to a bluish gray, I wanted to cry with both joy and misery at the same time. After a whole night of lying awake, staring into the darkness, I was as tired as death. But me and Laura were still alive. I reckoned that was something to be thankful for, even if it meant another eternal day of cooking for Pa and the boys.

I watched as Laura slid her legs out of bed and hobbled toward the hearth at the other end of the cabin. I don't know why, but I was awful glad to see things begin in the ordinary way they always did. I was glad for the kindling being stubborn to catch fire, as it always was. And for the soft clang of the iron teakettle being set on the hook. I didn't even mind when Mercy breathed loudly in my ear, "Wake up, Reb."

But cooking breakfast was a trial that morning.

Maybe it was on account of how tired we were, but I scorched the cornmeal making the corn mush, and Laura missed a pot of boiling water and dropped a handful of good sliced potatoes into the fire. We had to pull them out with a ladle, one by one. They were more than half burnt and covered in ashes.

Before we finished that, Pa and the boys came stomping in from the morning milking. Pa was raging to Amos about one of our cows who was in a fair way to die if she didn't have her calf soon. In Pa's eyes, it was all the cow's fault, of course. "Dumbest animals on earth," Pa said, taking off his boots and thumping them down on the floor. "She can just go on and die. Ain't that right, Amos? Let her lie out there suffering for a week and die. Never been nothing but trouble, that dumb old cow."

Pa didn't have no patience for weakness. When Ma died giving birth to Mercy, he hadn't been no different than he was about our cow. He said it was Ma's fault, that she just gave up and wanted to die. She would have taken the baby to die with her, too, but Mrs. Hawley had kept Mercy alive, nursing her and a baby of her own.

"Why ain't things ready on the table?" Pa said, giving us a scowl. "What the devil you two been doing all this time?"

"Everything's done, Pa," Laura answered, and we sent the food clattering onto the table in front of them. Half-burnt cornmeal mush, mashed potatoes, yellow pickles, fried pork, bread, and coffee.

"Git that bread down here to me—I'm hungry as a horse," Pa ordered. "And the potatoes. Where's the yeller pickles? This mush looks worse than death."

Pa always got his plate first.

Next it was Lorenzo, heaping his plate as if he was the only other one to eat. He was chattering on like a two-headed jaybird—talking about the Indian and what was gonna happen to him, and asking when the trial was going to be—and nobody was saying a word back.

Cousin George sat next to Amos, chewing his food silently. He always acted as if he was one of the lords of creation and never used more than two words in talking to us. "Cup's empty," he'd say loudly. Or, "Pork's cold."

George had come to live with us after he didn't get any land when his old father died—just two horses and a plow—but you would have thought he owned half a kingdom by the way he carried on.

In the middle of the meal, Pa waved his table knife at us.

"Over here," he said.

Me and Laura left the food we were watching on the hearth and came over to the table. I knew we were gonna hear about the cornmeal mush. Seemed as if there was always something that wasn't to Pa's liking.

"After we git done and you two git your breakfast," Pa told us through a mouthful of half-chewed food,

"I want you to go on upstairs and take the rest of this food, whatever scraps is left, to that Indian."

"What?" Laura gasped like a piece of wet wood in a hot fire.

I stared at Pa, and my face and arms felt suddenly prickly, as if I was being stuck with a thousand porcupine quills. Climb into the loft and take food to the murderer?

"Ain't no reason for the girls to do that, Pa," Amos said slowly, without looking up. "They got plenty of work in front of them. I'll take a dish of food and a slop jar upstairs for the Indian to use 'fore we head out to the fields."

Pa smacked his hand down on the table, making us all jump.

"Amos," he hollered. "You want your sisters to be a burden all your life? 'Cause that's exactly what they is gonna be." He pointed at us. "How they gonna be fit to live out here in the woods if they can't do nothing for themselves? They'll be jist like the Hawleys, who couldn't chop the head off a chicken to save their own lives."

Amos didn't answer a word, just started shoveling food fast into his mouth. Cousin George chewed on a piece of bread and grinned, like he found everything downright humorous. And Lorenzo said loudly, "Well, they ain't living with me. I ain't taking care of them when I'm old."

That made Pa laugh. He leaned over and smacked Lorenzo on the back. "You're the only one who's got brains," he said. "You can look after me in my old age. How 'bout that?"

While Pa was laughing, I let myself breathe again. I figured maybe he had just been trying to give us a fright. I know I ought to get used to such things from Pa. Our Ma always used to say, "Even eels get accustomed to being skinned"—but I don't reckon that's true.

Next to me, Laura gave a deep sigh and brushed her hands across her apron. "That all you wanted, Pa?" she said softly. When he didn't answer, we just turned back to our work as if we had never stopped—ladling out more food, clearing off dishes, and boiling water for washing.

But Pa didn't forget. As all of them were pulling on their boots to go out to the fields, he looked up suddenly and pointed his finger at us. We had just sat down with Mercy to have our little breakfast of green tea and bread.

"You remember what I told you about feeding that Indian," he said sharply. "He ain't had nothing to eat since we brought him here yesterday, so you take a dish of food up to him."

The bread I was eating stuck fast in my throat.

"Please don't leave us alone with him, Pa," Laura begged, her voice rising. "Me and Reb—we can't fight off Indians, truly we can't. If Indians come, me and Reb, we can't—"

"No Indians is gonna come here," Pa spat. "Don't be stupid fools. They know if any harm ever come to the Carvers, we'd kill every last one of them. And that Indian up there"—he grinned and gestured toward the chamber loft—"ain't going no place, not with how well he's chained. You just go on up and see for yourselves."

Pa opened the cabin door. "So I don't want to hear no more tears or complaining neither. I'm your Pa and you do what I says."

Laura didn't answer.

"You listenin'?" Pa hollered. "You hear what I said?"

"Yes, Pa," Laura whispered. And then Pa slid out the door like the mean old rattlesnake he was and disappeared.

After Pa left, Laura laid her head down on the table and wept so hard that it made me start to tremble with fear. Mercy sat in her chair staring silently at both of us, pale as a little snowdrop.

"What on earth are we gonna do, Reb?" Laura cried softly. "What on earth are we gonna do?" Watching her big shoulders heave up and down with sobs made my heart pound. I was dreadful afraid of being left alone in the world. If I lost Laura, what would happen to me?

After Ma died, I think my mind tried to turn Laura into my Ma. It erased and rewrote Laura and Ma, as if they were lines drawn on writing slates. But seeing my sister cry as if the world was ending made me realize that even though she was tall and strong for a girl, I could lose her just as quick and heartless as I had lost my Ma.

Taking a deep breath, I picked up one of the pewter dishes on the table.

"I'll go on upstairs," I said. "I don't much mind. I already seen that Indian once." I tried to keep my voice sounding as if I didn't much mind. I stood up and started to scrape the food from the dish into one of our big wooden bowls.

"Sit down," Laura answered, with her voice muffled in her arms. "You will not do any such thing, Reb."

I sank back down in my chair again and stared at my hands. I circled my fingers around one of my scrawny wrists and traced the lines on my palm so I wouldn't have to look over at Laura with her head down on the table.

Outside, a woodpecker rattled loudly on a tree. It was quiet above us in the loft, I noticed. No one would have guessed an Indian was up there. A gray mouse skittered across the plank floor, and I stomped my foot to make him run.

"All right," Laura said suddenly. She lifted her head and wiped a sleeve across her face. "You and me, we'll just go on up there and do exactly what Pa said. That Indian kills us, it'll be Pa's price to pay in heaven."

I didn't dare to get in her way. As she lumped food into the bowl, her lips were pressed tight to- gether. They made a fierce white line below her nose. "You're gonna carry the food," Laura said in a high-strung voice. "And I'm gonna walk behind you with a frying pan and a knife. That's what we are gonna do...."

So that's how we went up to the loft.

I had hold of the wooden bowl of leftover food, and Laura followed me with the frying pan. She had once kilt a rattlesnake with that same iron pan. Flung it right at the snake's head and smashed it flat. The rattlesnake tail had twelve bells on it, if you can be-lieve that, and we still had the tail and the frying pan both.

As we crept up the stairs, Laura hissed, "You just be sure to get out of the way." She was holding the pan so close behind me, seemed like I could feel its cold weight pressing on my neck. "If that Indian causes us any trouble, I'm throwing this frying pan at him," she said. "You hear me, Rebecca?"

I nodded.

from below
comes the girl
i have seen before—
the one with the darting eyes of the bird
and the shrieking voice of the jay.
Bird Eyes.
behind her, I see
a tall, older one.

Tall Girl Who Follows
carries a cooking pot
and a long knife
in her hands.
i close my eyes.
asleep.

the Bird Eye girl
flies toward me
like a gust of wind.
she leaves a bowl of food
at my feet and
runs.

the older one
stands still as a shadow.
sh-sh-sh-sh,
she whispers
like the trees.

i wait.
but Tall Girl Who Follows
does not move closer,
and she does not use
the sharp edge
of her long knife.

when I open my eyes,
they are gone.

Six

"Never been so full of fright in all my life," Laura said, pressing her hand to her chest when we reached the bottom of the stairs. "We just gave bread to the devil, sure enough we did." She squeezed my arm. "We was awful brave to do that, wasn't we, Reb? My heart was pounding like a hammer." She paused and looked at me. "How about yours?"

I nodded, and Laura leaned closer.

"You feeling scared?" she said, frowning. "You're being real quiet."

I shook my head no.

"Well, Pa never should have made us do that," she insisted. "It weren't right of him anyway. Even if the Indian was chained and all. He's a prisoner and a murderer. There was no cause for Pa to have his daughters take food up to him."

I don't think Laura felt a morsel of pity for the Indian after seeing him, not by the way she talked, and so I didn't dare to say how I felt. Ma always said I was too softhearted.

Sometimes Lorenzo or Cousin George brought back the chewed-off foot of a beaver or a fox that got out of one of their traps, and it turned my stomach over to see it. Or they'd grin and show me a broken-winged crow or something else that got caught instead. "Looka here at this," they'd say.

Although I hadn't noticed the chains when Lorenzo first sent me to the loft unawares, I couldn't shake from my mind the sight I had seen with Laura. The Indian was sitting on one of the straw-filled pallets that we kept in the loft. He had cuffs of iron fixed around both his ankles, right above his moccasins. A long piece of ox chain ran from the irons to a big bolt in the floor. Even though the Indian could move his arms and legs, I reckoned Pa was right—he would need to tear up half the plank floor to ever get away.

In the dim light of the loft, the man hadn't looked more than a few years older than Amos or Cousin George. There was a wide band of dark fur wrapped around his head, with a few tall feathers stuck on one side. Peculiar twists of hair dangled on each side of his face, and there were metal ornaments around his neck. Truth to speak, he appeared the way Amos or Cousin George might look in a nightmarish dream.

Still, even with how he looked, I couldn't help feeling pity for him being kept chained in our loft with the scuttling mice. And without much light to see or air to breathe. It seemed to me that the Indian could very well wither to dust and die sitting up there day after day.

I thought about those desperate foxes and beaver chewing off their own feet to survive. It made me shiver to imagine.

"You think Pa will keep him up there very long?" I asked Laura.

"I surely do hope not," Laura said, setting the frying pan back down on the hearth.

"How long?"

Laura sighed. "I don't know, Reb."

As I stacked the plates on the breakfast table, I said, "It's rather sorrowful seeing that Indian the way he is, with the chains and such. Don't you think?"

"What?" Laura stopped and stared at me as if I was addle-headed.

I hurried on. "I meant to say, it's dreadful sad seeing that Indian and knowing what he did. To that trapper."

"Yes," Laura said sharply, turning back to her work. "It's a terrible thing."

All day, I tried to turn the current of my mind to do more thinking about the Indian's terrible crime and less about the mournful sight I had seen upstairs. *The Indian murdered a man.* That's what I tried to tell my mind. And even though the murdered man was a trapper, and trappers were a miserable lot of men mostly, it was still an awful thing to do. Maybe the dead trapper had been a God-fearing and good-hearted man who didn't deserve to die just then. Maybe he had left behind ten children and a grieving wife. I tried hard to reason that the savage Indian deserved to be kept in our loft, chained to the floor. But it wasn't easy.

And the next morning when me and Laura went upstairs to fetch the wooden bowl we had left with the Indian, my mind grew even more tossed and turned. Because when I lifted up the empty bowl to carry it downstairs, I saw that there were six glass beads inside.

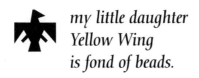

my little daughter
Yellow Wing
is fond of beads.

in her rabbit skin bag,
she carries
the tiny spirit berries.
nashké! nashké! she laughs.
look! look!
whitebluegreenred,
they catch the sun
and trickle through her small fingers
like drops of
rainbow water.

in the wooden bowl
left by Bird Eyes and
Tall Girl Who Follows,
i place
six tiny beads
from my moccasins.

four white. two blue.
the spirit berries
roll
back and forth,
back and forth.

a trade.

Seven

Seeing the beads in the center of our wooden bowl, I could not imagine how they had come to be there at first. For a moment, I thought they were little berries.

As I carried the bowl downstairs, I squinted at them, trying to imagine how it was possible. Where had berries, ripe or unripe, come from at the end of April? In Ohio? And how had they found their way into the bowl we had left upstairs with the Indian?

"What are you staring at?" Laura asked when we reached the bottom of the stairs.

On account of her bad eyes, I held the bowl higher. The glass beads rolled in tiny circles. "There's something inside the empty bowl," I replied. "Beads, I think. The Indian left us a handful of little beads."

"What?" Laura leaned closer.

"Ain't they pretty," I said, rocking the bowl gently so the glass beads turned and circled inside.

Pa was fond of saying that the Indians were so simple, they would trade everything they owned for a paltry handful of worthless trade beads. I had heard him tell folks that he could likely buy the whole state of Ohio—nay, the whole country—from the Indians for nothing but whiskey and blue glass beads if he was given half the chance.

But I had never seen any real Indian beads before, and I had to admit they were beautiful-looking things and maybe I would have given away something of my own to have them, too.

"Why would the Indian put beads inside our bowl?" Laura asked, rolling them back and forth with her finger.

"To thank us for bringing him food," I said. "Perhaps?"

Laura gave me a sharp look. "That's purely foolish nonsense, Reb."

"We gonna keep them?" I asked carefully.

Laura pressed her lips together. "You want to keep something from a murderer? What would the Lord in heaven think about that, Rebecca Ann Carver?"

"I don't see what's wrong with saving them," I answered, holding the beads in a small chink of sunlight.

"Ma would say it was wrong," Laura insisted. "Now wouldn't she, if she was alive?"

"I don't see why. How's keeping them gonna cause any harm?" I argued. "They didn't murder no one. They're nothing but a few glass beads."

I'm not sure why I wanted those beads so fiercely,

but I did. We didn't have many beautiful things of our own. Laura had a plain gold ring that belonged to our Ma, and a fine ivory comb from the East that was never used, and a piece of lace for her wedding gown someday. I had a silver teaspoon from Ma and a too-small pair of silk gloves. That was all.

Laura looked at me and heaved a sigh. "All right."

She turned the bowl on its side and poured the six beads into my hand. "But don't you dare tell Pa what I done," she said.

And now I could count six handsome beads from an Indian as mine.

each morning,
Bird Eyes and
Tall Girl Who Follows
bring me
a wooden bowl
filled with
salty meat,
bitter yellow fruits,
and coarse bread
made from
dirt and dust.

i do not
refuse
their food.
but i eat
slowly,
and i think of
deer meat sweet with maple sugar,
pumpkins boiled soft
in the fat of the bear,
and thick corn soup
at sunrise.

Eight

By the time another week had passed, our fears about being kilt by the Indian were hushed some. To my way of thinking, the Indian wouldn't give me and Laura gifts of beads and such if he was planning to bring any terrible harm on our heads. And if we were bringing him plates of food, perhaps he understood he needn't fear a thing from us either.

I began to go up to the loft by myself again to fetch the things we needed for our cooking. Me and Lorenzo were the only ones who could walk beneath the sloping roof without stooping over much. When I went up for onions or some apples for a pie, I would often give a sideways glance at where the Indian was sitting.

Seemed like I noticed something different about him each time. Something I hadn't seen before. "Do you know the Indian has a big piece of copper dangling from his neck?" I would tell Laura. "It's in the shape of a half-moon. I imagine it was from an old kettle, don't you think?"

Another morning, I noticed that the feathers on his head were hawk feathers, on account of how they were brown and square-shaped. And I saw he had two silver disks, the size of shillings, hanging from his earlobes.

I think Laura was as filled with curiosity as I was about the Indian. Every time I carried the empty bowl or dinner plate downstairs, she would hurry to ask what he had left for us. Sometimes it was beads, and other times it was odd and peculiar things like red-dyed porcupine quills or small tin cones with tufts of horsehair stuck inside. Once he even left a tarnished buckle that looked exactly like a little silver sun.

Still, Laura kept on worrying that Pa would find out about the gifts. "I should never have let you keep the beads in the first place," she fretted. "If Pa learns what I did, he will punish me so severely, I might as well go and shake hands with the devil himself. Our Ma would be downright ashamed with how I'm raising you. Downright ashamed."

I told Laura she was fine at raising me.

But I didn't tell her that I had started to give small things to the Indian, too.

i do not know why
the Bird Eye girl
leaves the nest
of the grass-weaving bird
near my moccasins.

or why she brings
the white flower
that heals sore eyes,
or the new green leaves
from the mouse-ear tree,
or one smooth brown acorn.

but i am pleased
to see them.

Nine

May 1812

When Mercy was being a pesky little bother one morning, I took out some of the beads and such for her to see. We kept all of the things from Indian John hidden in the chest at the foot of our bed. They were tucked underneath the embroidered pillowcases that Laura had stitched for her married life—when she found someone for marrying, that is.

Carefully, I put everything we had been given on the bed. They made a peculiar, colorful line. Mercy crawled onto the bed to watch and Laura perched on the edge of our wooden chest. She had just returned from the Hawleys, who had finally recovered their senses after two weeks of the fever.

"Look at this little quill, Mercy." I waggled one of the red–dyed ones in front of her. The quill reminded me of a long stem of meadow grass, with tiny white ridges where it appeared to have been bent and folded.

"Lemme see," Mercy demanded, reaching for it with her small fingers.

"Don't you ruin it," I said loudly, and Laura glared at me.

I picked up another quill and held it in my hand, studying it. "What do you suppose the Indians use them for?" I asked Laura.

My sister leaned closer. "Weaving, maybe?"

"Ain't porcupine quills round?" I rubbed the quill between my fingers. "All of these are flat."

Laura shrugged. "Perhaps the Indians make them that way."

"Or," I said, dangling the quill in front of Mercy's sour face, "maybe this here quill came from a flat red porcupine. You ever seen one of those in the woods before, Mercy, huh? Walking around like this on his flat red feet." I pretended to stomp across the floor while Mercy giggled and laughed.

And right at that moment—as I was stomping across the floor and we had beads and trinkets scattered all over our bedclothes—someone halloed outside our cabin door.

"Git the door, Reb," Laura hissed, scooping the beads and quills into her hands. "Quick, while I put these away."

I cast my eyes around the room to see what else was out of place. The table was a mess of bowls and dishes. The slop jar still sat by the door, waiting to be emptied. Where to set it? The only place I could see fit to hide it was in the corner next to our food cupboard. I tore off my apron and threw it over the jar for good measure.

Then I made a dash for the door before the visitor decided to set foot inside.

"Yes sir, begging your pardon," I said, opening the door halfway.

Outside stood a fellow who had all the appearances of a trapper. Unshaven face that hadn't seen a washbasin in weeks. Clothes that were nothing but shreds and patches. A sour smell coming off of him like clabbered milk. The fellow grinned at me and I saw that four of his teeth were missing in the front, as if he had lost them in an ear of corn.

"A sixpence to see the savage you got," he said, and held up a worn, old coin.

"What?" came flying out of my mouth before I could stop it.

"I says, miss," the fellow repeated slowly, "a sixpence for showing me the savage you got inside yer house." He waggled the coin in front of my eyes and grinned without his teeth. "Indian John."

A peculiar feeling came over me. I don't know why, but the sight of that trapper standing there with a sixpence sent a streak of anger right through me. I didn't want to let some ugly old trapper in our house so he could make a gazingstock out of Indian John. Wouldn't want people paying to stare at me—that's what I thought.

"No, matter of fact, you can't see the Indian, sir," I

said, trying to keep my voice polite and proper. "He ain't taking visitors today."

"What?"

Now it was the trapper's turn to look surprised. He narrowed his eyes and took a step closer to me, as if I was nothing but a little mosquito he was planning to swat out of the way. "Ain't Major Carver yer Pa?" he said sharply.

I nodded.

"Then you run and git him, girl. Stop vexing me—"

But at that moment, Laura appeared behind me. "Our Pa and the boys ain't here," she said, pulling herself up to her full height. Even the trapper seemed startled, looking her up and down again.

"Perhaps, if you don't mind, you could come back later." Laura wiped her hands on her apron, as if he had caught us in the middle of baking or cleaning.

"You Miz Carver, his wife?" the trapper said, turning his head to the side and spitting a stream of brown tobacco, half of which dribbled down his chin. He didn't seem in any real hurry to leave.

"Daughter," Laura answered. "I'm the oldest Carver daughter. Our Ma's dead. May her soul rest in peace." I knew that by saying this to the trapper, Laura meant to give him the idea that in the absence of Ma, she was the one taking charge.

"I ain't here to cause you two gals no trouble," the trapper said, making his voice sweet as tree sap. "Just want to get a glimpse at that captive Indian."

"We're in the middle of our baking," Laura said.

"Ain't gonna stay for more than one half minute."

Me and Laura didn't have any choice, seemed

like, but to let him in. We couldn't stand in the way of a grown man. Not if Pa got word of it. So, the trapper scraped his boots on the stone beside the door and pushed his way right inside. I could see his eyes darting from one thing to the next, taking account of everything we had—the pewter on the table, our big food cupboard, the red-painted chest from the East that sat at the foot of Pa's bed—

"Indian's upstairs," Laura said, trying to hurry him on his way.

It wasn't long after the trapper went up the narrow steps that I knew something was wrong. There was a thumping noise, as if a large stone had been dropped on the floor, and then came the sound of the trapper's raspy old laughter. A sickly feeling crawled right into my stomach.

I couldn't hear all the words the trapper was saying to Indian John, but the few I could catch were ugly enough. There was more raspy laughter and scraping and thumping on the floor above our heads, as if the trapper was tormenting poor Indian John, who was desperate to move.

What happened next took me by surprise, though. Laura ran to the hearth, picked up the big frying pan, and flew up the steps to the loft.

"Out of our house," she hollered at the trapper in a voice that didn't even sound like her own. It was loud and booming, as if she was shouting into a barrel. "Out of our house before I smash you to bits."

And believe me, by the sound of her voice, there was no question that she would smash the trapper's head flat as a rattlesnake's if given half the chance. I expect that the trapper must have believed this, too, because he left the loft so fast, he missed half of the steps coming down.

While he was shooting past me and out the door, I noticed that he had something in his hand. It looked like maybe it was a twist of brown paper, but I didn't pay it any real notice. I just stood by the hearth, with my knuckles squeezed white, praying for the cabin door to close and for us to be rid of him.

After the trapper had gone, Laura came back down the stairs. She didn't even glance in my direction. All she said was, "May the Lord forgive me for defending the life of a murderer," and she dropped the pan on the hearth with a loud clang that made me jump. "And may the Lord keep Pa from finding out what I done, too," she added.

Then she picked up a lump of bread dough we had left on the table and began to knead it furiously, as if she was trying to squeeze the life out of it.

"Any harm come to him?" I said finally.

"To whom?" Laura answered.

"Indian John."

Laura's hands stopped right in the middle of her work. "Don't you show even the smallest kindness or pity for that Indian, Rebecca Carver," she said fiercely. "Or I will take all of the things that you've hidden in our chest—the quills, the beads, everything—and I will burn them to ashes this very minute."

Laura lifted up the dough and thudded it back on the table, lifted and thudded—hard enough to send up clouds of flour. To my way of thinking, she wasn't making the smallest bit of sense. First she saved Indian John from the no-good trapper and then she scolded me for asking a trifling question.

"I only wanted to know," I kept on.

With the way Laura's eyes looked daggers at me, I didn't dare to open my mouth again. I didn't dare to ask if she saw the trapper carrying something when he left the loft, or if she thought he had stolen something from us or from Indian John.

I just kept silent and did my work without a word. By evening, I had nearly forgotten all about the trapper. I didn't know then what an unfortunate mistake that would later turn out to be.

the trapper
steals from me
as the crow steals
from a patch of corn.

i can smell a trapper coming
upwind
in a rainstorm
two camps away.

the trapper laughs
and plucks a feather from my head,
laughs
and struts as if he is
ten feet tall
in his boots,
too tall to fit
in his own canoe.

holding the feather
in his hand, he turns
and runs.

cowardly gichi-mookomaan,
i whisper,
you could steal

the wings
from the soaring eagle,
but it would not make you
strong
or brave.

Ten

After the no-good trapper, a whole river of people started coming to our door to see Indian John. It was as if the trapper had opened the waterways of curiosity and folks arrived from far and wide to stare at a captive Indian.

I didn't care for their visits at all.

Amos had once told me about Learned Pig shows, where people paid a few cents to see an exhibition where real pigs spelled and counted. He said that some of the pigs had even been taught to spell the name of the president of the United States—Mr. Madison himself.

I wasn't sure all that was true.

But it seemed to me that the families who came to our house acted as if we had a Learned Pig show inside. The women arrived wearing their best going-to-meeting gowns, and the children always carried something to give us Carvers. Since it was the time of year when most folks didn't have much good food left, it was most often a pail of butter or a few brown eggs—as if we were foolish enough not to have cows or chickens of our own.

After they stepped inside, the women would cast their eyes around our cabin and say in a jumpy voice, "That Indian ain't allowed free, is he? You've got him in chains now, I suppose?"

If it was up to me, I would have told them the Indian was sitting by the fire sharpening his hatchet. See how fast that would make them throw on their bonnets, turn on their heels, and run. Let them leave Indian John and us alone.

But Pa would certainly hear of it and give me a thrashing. He had given Laura an awful hard scolding when he got word of how she had treated that miserable trapper.

So me and Laura didn't have any choice but to tell the visitors where to find Indian John chained in the loft. Then they would go up the narrow stairs, real slowly, still talking to us as they went up. Always the women in front and their children behind, clutching hold of their skirts.

After a period of silent staring, when we could just hear the feet of the children shuffling back and forth on the floor, they would often holler down to us.

"He's asleep. When's he wake up?"

Truth to speak, I think Indian John just pretended to be asleep. When he heard footsteps, I think he would lean his head down as far as it would go on his chest, so the only things visible in the shadows were the bottoms of his moccasins, his stretched-out legs, and the top of his head.

"Can you git him to wake up?" they'd ask.

Me and Laura would give each other a look, and then one of us would holler upstairs that we didn't care to do anything to make the Indian angry. That usually sent the curious eyes hurrying back down from the loft.

Sometimes, though, they got to throwing things at Indian John, trying to wake him up. They threw little things mostly, like the kernels of dried corn that were scattered on the floor of the loft. Or something the children had carried in. Maybe a clay marble or a pebble. From below, we could hear things clattering and rolling across the floor. The children would holler, "Hit him right there on the shoulder, you see that, Ma?" and they would laugh and clap. It always brought a terrible sick feeling to my stomach.

They were only throwing corn kernels and pebbles, but it seemed like I could feel the sting of every single piece that they threw as if it was my own skin instead of Indian John's. I could scarcely understand how people could think to do such things.

Me and Laura tried to keep the loft swept as best we could. After the visitors left, I often went upstairs and swept again. If Laura wasn't minding me, I would leave something small near Indian John's feet to try and make up for what folks had done.

Once I left him a brown butterfly wing I found near the springhouse. And another time, a scrap of green silk ribbon I had saved since Ma's death.

Sometimes, before I went back downstairs, I would whisper that I was real sorry for the way people were. I expect that he didn't understand a word, but I felt better for saying it.

After seeing what a gazingstock they made of Indian John, I never wanted to go to a Learned Pig show. Not even when I was old. It seemed to me that it wasn't right to stare at anything, human or animal, in a show. Even if it was only trained pigs who could spell the name of the president.

Eleven

A different sort of visitor arrived one morning during the second week of May. Me and Laura were boiling clothes outside. We had a roaring good fire going and a mess of clothes to wash in the big kettle.

In the field just across the road from our cabin, Pa and the men were burning the last of the big brush heaps they had piled up in the fall. You could smell the bitter–sharp smoke from the burning wood on the air. Spring was a peculiar time, I thought. Sweetness and bitterness both. We tapped the sweetness out of some trees and burnt others to pieces within the same few months.

I squinted at the field, trying to see where Pa and the men were working, and that's when I spotted someone coming down the road.

All I saw at first was a blaze of copper red hair on

a stranger who looked as skinny as a beanpole. His brown coat flapped loosely around him as he walked, and he carried his hat in one hand.

"Now who could that be?" Laura said.

"Likely someone else coming to stare at Indian John," I sighed. "Or to bother us about his trial."

Pa had said that Indian John's trial would be held at the beginning of June, after the corn was in the ground. But I was awful tired of answering folks' eternal questions about it. Or perhaps I didn't like to be reminded that Indian John was still accused of murder.

"We aren't fit for visitors. Look at us." Laura tried to push her loose straggles of hair underneath her cap, and she told me to pull down my rolled-up sleeves. "Mind your manners, Reb," she whispered.

When the stranger reached us, he stopped nearly a dozen feet away. Looking up, I tried to give him what I thought was a tired, unfriendly stare. As if we were too busy to be bothered to help him.

"Good morning," he said awkwardly, twisting the brim of his black hat in his hands like he was full of nerves.

He looked to be about the same age as Amos or Cousin George. His frock coat was rather worn and ill fitting, with one button missing. And the cloth around his neck was tied in a clumsy knot. But his wavy red hair was combed real carefully to one side, I noticed. It curled a little in the early morning dampness, and he reached up with one hand to smooth it down.

"My name is Peter Kelley," he said in a stumbling voice. "Mr. Peter Kelley. From Warren, Ohio."

I could tell by the way Laura was trying to straighten her day cap that she was taken by him. He did have kind brown eyes, I would venture to say, and a gentle sort of appearance with his skinny shoulders and his too-large coat.

"Perhaps I've come to the wrong place," he stammered. He cast a look at our cabin, then at the clearing around us. "I have, haven't I?" He glanced at Laura, and I could see his face grow a shade of pink. Truthfully, we were both water-splattered and wearing our oldest gowns.

"They told me the Carvers would have the biggest log house in the settlement, so that's how I would know where I was," he continued. "And this was the biggest house I saw, so I thought perhaps this was the right one. But now it seems I've come to the wrong place...." The stranger's voice trailed away and he looked suddenly uncomfortable and unsure of what to do next. The hat turned around and around in his hands.

"This here's the Carvers'," my sister said shyly, nodding in the direction of our house. "I'm Miss Carver. This here's Rebecca." She pointed at me. "Have you come on business with our Pa?" she asked.

"Well, no...." The stranger's voice faltered. "As it happens, I was hoping, if I might—well, if he's still here, that is—to speak to Amik."

A little ripple of laughter escaped out of my mouth and my hand flew up to my lips to cover it. Laura gave me a glare and told the fellow that, begging his pardon, there was no one in our family called by that name. She motioned in the direction of the field where the men were working and told the gentleman that perhaps he could find someone there to provide him some help.

Mr. Kelley appeared as lost as a young boy. "You haven't heard of Amik? Truly?" he said, running his fingers through his hair. "The Indian is no longer a captive here?"

Now, I had never heard our Indian called anything but Indian John. No one had ever uttered the name Amik for him. The sound of it put me in mind of a bird calling in the trees. *Ah-mick, Ah-mick.* Where had the man been told such a peculiar name? I wondered.

Laura wiped her hands on her apron and told Mr. Kelley to please forgive our bad manners—that, begging his pardon, we didn't understand exactly who he was looking for. "Pa and the men call our Indian by the name Indian John," she explained. "He's kept in irons in our loft for murdering a man."

But I nearly fell into the wash kettle when I heard what Mr. Kelley said next.

"I'd be very obliged to speak to your Indian if I might, Miss Carver," he told Laura, in a soft voice that was almost pleading in its sound. He looked down and the hat turned around and around in his pale, skinny hands. "I believe that Amik—Indian John—is perhaps an old acquaintance of mine."

when Red Hair climbs the stairs
to see me,
all appears as a dream.

neejee! neejee!
my friend! my friend!
i say.

i see that
Red Hair is tall now,
tall and thin
as a young sapling tree,
but his hair
is still the color
i remember from long ago—
the vermilion color that does not
wash away.

Red Hair grins and makes a picture
with his hands—
do you remember the river, Amik?
near my Pa's old house? remember?

i laugh.
eya′, yes,
i tell Red Hair—
i taught you to swim there
in the time of ripe corn.

Red Hair grins
and shakes his head.
no, you did not teach me,
he says—
you put me on your back
and dove!

i tell my friend
it is the way the Ojibbeways learn
to swim
like fish.

Red Hair laughs and says,
remember our games of moccasin
and sticks
and my Pa teaching you
to play the fiddle?
eya', eya', I say,
yes, yes.

we grow silent.
below
i can hear Bird Eyes
and Tall Girl Who Follows
clattering and shuffling
as they do.

Red Hair asks
in a soft voice,

Amik—
did you do what they say?

i close my eyes
and remember
the day
the cool green river water
pushed us upward
like two strong arrows
shot into blue sky.

old friend,
i sigh,
how we have
changed.

Twelve

"He's real handsome-looking, isn't he?" Laura whispered after Mr. Kelley had gone up the stairs. "Never saw him in the settlement before, have you?"

"You think he's truly acquainted with Indian John?" I asked.

Laura shook her head. "No, I don't see how. Still"—she gave a half smile and smoothed her apron with her hands—"I think it would be kind to ask him to stay for tea, don't you? For all his troubles?"

But as we got out the tin of tea and set the water to boil, I think it gave both of us a jolt when we suddenly realized that Mr. Kelley was talking with Indian John upstairs. *Talking.* And his voice was speaking in words that were no longer English.

At first, me and Laura just stared wide-eyed at the ceiling planks above our heads, still as two stones.

•69

The strange sound of the voices mumbling back and forth was enough to frighten a person near to death. Our kettle bubbled over and hissed onto the fire. All the while Mercy tugged the bed quilts off our bed, but we didn't move from where we stood.

"You think I should run and get Amos from the field?" I whispered to Laura.

But then, just as suddenly as it had started, the conversation in our loft stopped. Mr. Kelley came down the stairs slowly. I watched him hesitate on the last step and glance back up, as if he had changed his mind and would turn around, even though he didn't.

Laura stared at me, uncertain what to do. "Mr. Kelley—" she began in a halting voice. "We've made tea if you'd like some. I don't know if you were intending to stay or not."

Mr. Kelley gave us a startled look. I was nearly sure that he was going to say no, by the wary expression on his face. But then, quite suddenly, his face softened, and he nodded a little.

"Thank you, Miss Carver," he said, coming over to the table. "Thank you, I'll have a small cup of tea, yes." Awkwardly, he pulled up a chair and sat down at our big table. He was all elbows and knees and couldn't seem to decide where to set his hat until he finally put it on the floor near his feet.

"So has Ami—Indian John—been here long, in your Pa's cabin?" Mr. Kelley asked in a curious voice while we fixed tea for him. Since he was company, my sister gave him our only unchipped teacup and put some of our best loaf sugar on the table.

"About three weeks," Laura answered. "My Pa and

the other men brought him here near the end of April." Then she added carefully, "How are you acquainted with him, Mr. Kelley?"

I held in my breath, waiting for his answer.

"Well . . ." The man paused and stared down at his folded-up hands. "When I was ten or eleven years old, growing up east of here, the two of us were friends."

"Friends?" came flying out of my mouth.

Mr. Kelley looked at me in a way that reminded me of Amos when he thought I had said something foolish. "Yes, we were good friends," he repeated.

He told us that Amik's father was the chief of a small band of Chippewas. "Ojibbeways, as they call themselves," he said. Mr. Kelley described how the Indians used to return every spring from their maple sugar grounds and stay on his Pa's land through the summer. He glanced at Laura and asked her if she had ever heard of the Nibinishi River, in the eastern part of Ohio, but she shook her head no.

"Well, the band always came to fish on our river, as they had done for years and years, I suppose, long before we had come," he explained.

Mr. Kelley said that Amik and some of the other Indians were near to his age. "I had four brothers when I was growing up," he told us. "And we would play games and run all day with Amik and the other boys when our chores were done. I was quick with languages. My Pa said I had an ear for it. So, I learned to speak with them as well as anyone."

I could hardly even imagine the scene in my mind—our own Ma opening up the door of our cabin and letting us play with Indian children. Even Laura gave a surprised gasp. "Your Pa and Ma? They allowed you to do that?"

Mr. Kelley studied his cup of tea, as if he was thinking hard. "Indians aren't—well, they aren't, forgive me for saying this—" He paused and stumbled over his words. "Well, it is my belief—and it was my Pa's belief, too—that Indians are as human as white men. Truthfully, in a great many respects, they are, Miss Carver," he stammered. "And in some ways, more so."

There was an uncomfortable long silence after he spoke. I drank a big gulp of tea and peered over the top of my cup at my sister Laura, but I didn't dare to breathe a word about all of the things Indian John had given to us. Or how I sometimes thought Indians were human, too.

"I don't see how the murder of innocent folks can be counted as human, Mr. Kelley," Laura said finally, in a strong voice that echoed Ma's Bible-reading one. "Even if he was once your friend, how can you call his actions human?"

"No, certainly not," Mr. Kelley answered quickly. "But perhaps what everyone believes—" Mr. Kelley hesitated and looked down at the table. "Perhaps, well, perhaps it isn't all true," he finished.

I stared at Mr. Kelley.

Even Laura seemed startled. "Are you saying that our Pa's Indian didn't kill the trapper?" she said.

"I don't know what to think, truly I don't," Mr. Kelley answered, rubbing his eyes wearily. "Amik was always a good friend. For all the years we were growing up. He was never the kind to—"

Right at that moment, Pa and the boys came stomping through the doorway. Me and Laura were so taken by surprise, we nearly knocked over our chairs in our rush to stand up.

First thing Pa said, of course, was that nobody came out to the field to tell him there was a fellow here to see him, and he gave me and Laura a hard look. After that, he sat down at the table and announced that he was Major Carver—and as the major general of this part of Ohio, it was his duty to ask the fellow what business he had in our settlement.

Mr. Kelley's narrow face turned as pink as a spring wildflower and his elbow sent his spoon clattering to the floor. "I'm Mr. Peter Kelley, Esquire," he managed to say, trying to reach for his spoon. "I'm an acquaintance of the Chippewa Indian you have caught for murder—"

"Acquaintance?" Pa's voice was sharp.

Mr. Kelley took a deep breath. I could see his shoulders rise up and down, and I felt sorry for him because of my Pa being the way he is.

"I'm newly in the practice of law," he said real quiet. "And I have come to see about perhaps defending him in his trial."

My mouth just about fell to my feet when I heard that. All he had told us was that he was acquainted with the Indian from boyhood. He never breathed a word about defending him. Or being a lawyer.

My Pa let out a loud hoot of laughter. "Well, don't that beat all," he said, smacking his hand down on the table. "George," he hollered at my no-good cousin. "George—this man is gonna stand up for a savage. Don't that beat all you ever heard?"

Cousin George grinned and shook his head.

"You a real lawyer?" Pa asked.

"Yes," Mr. Kelley answered, as red as beets.

"You study many books?"

"Yes," Mr. Kelley said.

"Well, I'll tell you what." Pa snorted and leaned forward. "You got more ed–u–cation than you got brains, Mr. Peter Kelley, Esquire. Everybody around here knows that savage up there"—Pa jabbed his finger toward the loft—"kilt a poor fellow who didn't have no reason to die. Kilt him in cold blood with a tomahawk." He fixed his eyes on Peter Kelley's face. "And if you keep that Indian up there from hanging for his crime, you got the fewest brains of any man I know on this green earth."

Pa stood up and pointed at the door. "Now git out of my house."

Seems like when a person is treated poorly by someone else, it makes you want to take their side. I don't know why. Maybe it isn't even a side you would have picked under other circumstances.

I couldn't imagine how Peter Kelley was going to stand up to my Pa. Or how he was going to save an Indian who everybody believed was guilty. But as I watched Mr. Kelley pick up his hat and walk out the door with his skinny shoulders and his too–big coat, I am ashamed to say that I wanted to see him try.

Thirteen

I didn't expect that Peter Kelley would ever dare to come back to our house. Not with how Pa had run him off. While we fixed supper that night, I asked Laura, "You think he'll still try to be the lawyer for Indian John?"

"Perhaps," Laura said, keeping her eyes on the turnips she was cutting.

"You think all he told us is true? About Indian John not being the kind of person to kill a trapper?"

"I know what our Pa and the other men have said," she answered evenly. "That's what I know to be true."

I felt sorry for Laura. She had been real quiet and downcast ever since Pa had sent Mr. Kelley away and scolded us. I figured she had taken a small fancy to the lawyer just in the brief moment we had met him. On account of his wavy red hair and gentle eyes, I think. And I expect he would have made a good beau for her if he hadn't been going against our Pa and defending an Indian.

Pa always said the only man who would ever marry Laura was an old widower. "Someone who ain't interested in picking through all the apples in the barrel and will take jist about anyone. That's the fellow for you," Pa would tell her. But I knew that kindhearted Laura would make a good wife for anyone.

"You suppose Mr. Kelley knows something about Indian John that Pa don't?" I kept on. "That why he's trying to defend him?"

"I don't know," Laura answered, standing up and dumping her handful of turnips into the soup pot. "But he has some very peculiar beliefs about Indians."

"Maybe Indian John didn't murder anyone— couldn't that be true?" I said. "Maybe they caught the wrong person by mistake. Don't that happen sometimes?"

Laura's eyes flashed toward me. "You better not let Pa catch you saying something like that, Rebecca Ann Carver," she warned. "That's spreading lies and gossip."

I tried to put my restless questions in the back of my mind, but it wasn't easy. While we did our mending work in the evening, I thought hard about the new calf that had finally been born to our sickly cow and what we could name it if it lived long enough. I tried to remember the words to a verse that Ma always used to recite. But my mind still circled back to Indian John and Peter Kelley. What did

Mr. Kelley know? What had he said to Indian John in the loft?

Laura kept her head down and her eyes fixed on her work the whole time. She didn't speak hardly a word. When Amos told me they would need help in the fields the next day, I was glad for the chance to go and leave Laura to herself.

The next morning, I followed Pa and the boys out to the fields. It was a real pretty morning. The wispy clouds looked like bits of wool tumbling across the cabin floor. Under my feet, the dirt was cool and soft. Only thing Pa said to me was that I had better work as hard as a boy.

In the field, I stayed close to Amos and far from the others. He had a pointed ax for loosening the rocks and roots, and I tugged the smaller ones out of the dirt and threw them in a pile. The field had to be cleared—grubbed, as the men said—before it could be plowed for corn.

It was hard not to talk and fill up the empty space when you were working with Amos. He could go for hours without saying anything, stopping only to spit or take a swig of water from the jug he had set into the field dirt.

One thing I found while I was grubbing was an arrowhead point.

I thought at first it was a stub of a sprouting plant, and then when I leaned closer, I realized it was a small gray arrowhead. I held it in my palm for Amos to see.

"Here, see what I dug up."

"Lorenzo's got a whole collection of those," he said, not even taking a half minute to look at it. "The field's full of them."

"I never found one before," I said, surprised. "How'd they get here, in our field?"

"How do you think, Reb?" Amos went back to chopping at the dirt. "This was Indian land long before it was ours. How do you reckon arrowheads got here?"

Finding that arrowhead had a powerful effect on me because I had never before thought about Indians living on the same ground where we lived now. In my mind, they had always been on the far side of the Crooked River or on the edges of wherever we were living. Indian lands were always beyond— beyond the river, beyond that mountain, on the other side of that lake. They had their place. We had ours. And it had never been the same place. But looking at that little gray–colored arrowhead gave me a peculiar feeling.

My mind started thinking about how it would feel if, in the years to come, someone dug up something from us Carvers—a button, or a spoon that got thrown out with the dishwater, or a musket ball. Would they know we had lived here? That this had been our farm? Or would we be just like the Indian who sent this arrow flying? Would we be forgotten and long gone?

I remembered how Ma's bones were buried on this land, under a big hickory tree that she always loved. In a hundred years, if they dug under that tree, would they know whose bones—

I dropped the arrowhead back into the dirt and

pressed the clods down hard with my bare feet to cover it. Didn't want to think about that old arrowhead and the Indians anymore. My head was a mixed-up jumble.

We grubbed rocks and roots the whole day, from morning to evening. By the time Pa was ready to go in for the supper meal, my arms were pink from the sun, and my palms looked as if they had been rubbed across a grindstone.

Lorenzo didn't take any pity on me. "Looka there at that little pile of stones you done," he said, coming over. "The pile of stones me and George have is twice the size of yours." He reached down to tug a fist-sized rock out of the ground. "You missed this one," he said, sending it clattering onto my pile.

I scowled at him. "Maybe you and Cousin George ought to stay out here and find all of the rest of them rocks yourself."

After Lorenzo kicked a footful of dirt in my direction and ran off, I had to admit that it didn't look like me and Amos had done very much. That was the problem with grubbing out the fields. You worked for hours and hours, and it seemed as if all the same stones and roots came back. No matter how far you flung them or how fast you dug them up, you couldn't get rid of them. The earth was stubborn. That was the truth.

I guess Peter Kelley must have been the same way. He wouldn't give up easily. No matter what my mean Pa said. Because when we returned to the house in the evening, Laura pulled me outside and whispered real low, "Today, while you and the boys was gone in the fields, Peter Kelley stopped by here."

Red Hair climbs the steps
a second time
to see me.

i close my eyes.

you are a stranger now,
i tell him.
go away, gichi-mookomaan,
and do not return
again.

Red Hair says it has been
many winters
and we have been separated
far apart,
but two things he has not forgotten,
one
is how we saved his ma, and
two
is the stories of the Old Ones.

he says to me—
Amik, do you remember
your grandmother's old story
of the Fox, Snake, and Man?

i know the story well—

many strings of lives ago,
Little Fox risked his life
to save Man
from the coils of a great serpent.
but as time passed,
one winter to the next,
one winter to the next,
Man forgot Fox's good deed,
as he forgets many things.

one starving moon,
Man drew his sharp knife
to kill
poor thin Fox who had eaten
from his cache of winter food.
don't you remember me?
Fox cried.
don't you
remember?

do you see? Red Hair says—
i am taking your side.
i do not want to be
the man
who forgot

•81

what the fox had done.

i am silent
for a long while
thinking of Fox and Man
and the great serpent.

finally, i tell him—
Red Hair,
no matter what the gichi-mookomaanag
say about me—
Amik is not guilty.

Fourteen

Laura wouldn't tell me anything else about Peter Kelley's visit until the next morning when Pa and the boys left to hitch up our horse. Even then, she wouldn't breathe a word until she had gone outside and made certain they were inside the barn.

After she closed the cabin door, she turned toward me and spoke in a whisper. "I was so startled when I saw that it was Mr. Kelley yesterday. I didn't know whether or not I ought to let him in."

"What did he say?"

Laura took a deep breath. "Well, he was full of nerves, I could tell. You shoulda seen the way his face was flushed, as if he had a fever. And he talked so fast I could hardly keep up. But he said he knew our Pa believed in his heart that Indian John had murdered someone—and maybe he had—but he wasn't certain himself and so all he wanted to do was talk to Indian John, just talk for a while, and try to find out the truth."

Laura looked at me, wide-eyed. "I was wrong to go against Pa and let him in, wasn't I?"

"Not so long as Pa don't find out." I grinned.

Laura straightened her shoulders and pressed her lips together. "Well, I did let him in, even if it was wrong." Her voice fell to a softer whisper. "And he brought me a little handful of spring violets, too," she added.

"Violets?"

"Over here." She led me to our wooden chest. "I put them inside with our other things." Sure enough, inside our chest was a knot of flowers from the woods. Delicate purple ones. Me and Laura dearly loved violets.

"I know I shouldn't have taken them," she whispered. "But no one ever gave me a thing like that before, and I didn't know what to do, truly I didn't. Aren't they beautiful, Reb?" She lifted them up from the teacup of water where they were setting, and my heart pounded, fearing that Pa and the boys might come stomping in.

"Maybe you shouldn't keep them," I told her in a jumpy voice. My eyes darted from the flowers to the cabin door and back again.

"Reb Carver, I daresay you should be the one to talk, with all the things you have kept from the Indian," Laura whispered loudly. "My little flowers won't do any harm, I don't think." She set the violets carefully back in their teacup and closed the heavy wooden cover. "Never got flowers from a gentleman before," she said, smoothing her hand across the top of the chest. "Even if Mr. Kelley is helping a savage Indian, they're still real nice."

I didn't say a word, just hoped in my head that Mr. Kelley was smart enough to know that he could get me and Laura in awful bad trouble with Pa if he kept coming around to our house and didn't watch his step.

Standing up, Laura cast her eyes around the cabin and sighed. "I surely hope he doesn't come back this morning," she said. "What would he say about me keeping a house like this?"

"He's gonna come back?" I asked, wide-eyed.

Laura tugged Mercy off the bed and began picking up the yarn that she had unrolled every which way. "He said he might, if Pa and the boys are gone."

I already knew that they were going to the mills with the last of our shelled corn. After they had the wagon ready, they would rattle down the road with our old horse, Mary Ester. She walked so slow and plodding, I knew they wouldn't be back from the mills until well after dark.

Sure enough, not long after they left, we heard the sound of a person coming down the path toward the house. Me and Laura both jumped up from our baking, and Laura nearly spilled a whole jug of water in her rush to scrub the dough and flour off her hands.

When we reached the door, Peter Kelley stood outside waiting. He was wearing the same wide-brimmed hat and ill-fitting coat. "Good morning," he said, pulling the hat off his head real fast and turning a shade of pink, I noticed.

Laura answered "Good morning" in a soft voice that didn't even sound like her own. "This here's my sister Rebecca," she told Mr. Kelley as if he had never seen me before. Strange to say, this time he had a single snowshoe tucked under his arm.

i hold the snowshoe
from Red Hair
in my hand
and touch the smooth curve
of the wood
made from the straight white tree
that grows strong snowshoes.

my fingers trace
the paths of the netting
woven tight as bowstrings
by Rice Bird's quick wooden needle.

Red Hair asks me—
did you wear this snowshoe
in the moon of the Big Spirit?
in the moon of the sucker fish?
in the moon of the crust on the snow?
eγa', eγa', eγa',
γes, γes, γes,
i sigh.

i do not see why my friend asks such
foolish questions—

how does he think
i would walk
in the winter moons,
when the snow

is deep
and the freeze
is hard?

Red Hair says
he is asking
for the trial,
that is the reason
for his questions.

i tell him
i do not see
why the white man's trial
will need
my snowshoes.

Fifteen

When Peter Kelley finished his meeting with Indian John and came down the stairs, Laura invited him to stay for a piece of custard pie.

She had made the pie the day before, just in case Mr. Kelley did come back again as he had promised. But Laura said that I was the only person, in all of earth and heaven, who was to know that she had used up eight whole eggs, four great spoonfuls of precious loaf sugar, and a good bit of our nutmeg to make it.

I believe that Peter Kelley didn't know what to answer at first. After Laura asked him to stay, he stumbled over his words. First saying no, he didn't want to cause us any trouble with our Pa, and then saying perhaps he could stay for a moment to be polite, and finally deciding that it was a real kind offer and, yes, he would greatly appreciate a piece of pie.

"It's one of our Ma's good pies," Laura told him. "The kind she used to make."

"Your Ma?" Peter Kelley asked gently as he sat down at the table. "She is gone?"

"Three years ago," Laura answered. "She died in the month of March. God rest her soul."

"Right after giving birth to our sister Mercy," I added, nodding at Mercy, who had her fingers in the yarn basket again. I don't know why I always had to tell folks that our Ma had died giving birth to her, but I did. It sounded as if I was putting all of the blame for Ma's death on my helpless little sister, who was born into this world silent and nearly blue. Maybe I still was.

"I don't have any sisters of my own, only brothers," Mr. Kelley said, slowly stirring the tea that Laura had set in front of him. "Just two brothers still living now and my Ma, who has grown quite old and feeble, I'm afraid." He shook his head, and I could tell his Ma was dear to him by the sorrowful way his face looked.

"Every time I see Amik here, what I can't keep from thinking about is how . . ." He paused and looked toward the loft stairs. "Is how my Ma wouldn't be alive today—she wouldn't have raised any of us, not my brothers or me—if it weren't for his family." He pointed upward, as if pointing straight at Amik himself. "Years ago, his family saved her life."

"What?" I said, more loudly than I should have.

He glanced at Laura and me. "I could only have been nine or ten years old when it happened," he said. "It was the fall of the year, I remember, and we had all gone to a cranberry marsh to pick berries."

In my mind, I could picture a cranberry marsh—the green color of the leaves and the bright red berries nestled inside like jewels.

Peter Kelley continued. "All of us went—my Pa and Ma and my four brothers. I remember how it was a beautiful autumn afternoon, not a hint of a cloud. All was right with the world, it seemed. That's what I remember most about that day." He wrinkled his forehead. "Do you understand what I mean?"

I nodded.

There was a summer afternoon before Ma died that I had not forgotten either. It was a real pretty day. Me and Laura and Ma were picking beans in the garden, and we got to singing songs and tossing beans from one basket to another, just for our own amusement. We had never done a thing like that before, and we must have been a sight. I could still recall the bright blue sky and the sound of Ma laughing.

Peter Kelley shook his head. "Maybe we weren't watching as close as we should have been, on account of how beautiful that day was. But before any of us knew what had happened, a rattlesnake came through the cranberries, just came up real sudden, and it struck our Ma hard on the foot."

I caught my breath. I had seen more than my share of rattlesnakes, and I knew what they could do to folks if you came across them unawares.

Peter Kelley closed his eyes, as if he was remembering the scene exactly as it was. "I can still hear the terrible sound of Ma's voice shrieking for us. Pa sent me and my brother Nathaniel running for the nearest town to fetch a doctor. Never ran so fast in all my life," he said softly, "trying to save my Ma that morning."

I swallowed hard, thinking about my own Ma.

"The doctor told us to bind up her foot with tobacco leaves to draw out the poison. If the swelling grew worse, he said to dig a hole in the ground and have her put her foot inside the dirt, packed in tobacco leaves.

"We tried everything." Peter Kelley shook his head. "But Ma's foot and leg swelled up as full as the skin could hold. It was black from the poison, truly it was." He took a deep breath. "We knew she wasn't long for the earth. Not more than a few days left, everyone told us. And we didn't know how we would manage in the world without her. My youngest brother was only four."

I cast a look at Laura because I remembered this feeling too well.

Peter Kelley continued. "The next day my older brother met a Chippewa man fishing in our river. All of us could speak some words in Chippewa, and my brother the best of all, so my brother told the Indian—" Peter's voice caught in his throat. "He told him about the coming death of our poor Ma.

"That same evening," Peter Kelley said, "I heard a soft knock on our door, and I opened it to see who it was. Amik's grandmother stood outside in the darkness." He squinted his eyes. "All these years later, I can still recall exactly what she looked like. She was called by the name Old Turtle Woman, and I remember how she was a small woman with stooped shoulders and gray-streaked hair, and how she always wore a circle of tiny rabbit bones around her neck.

"The woman pressed a bundle of leaves toward me, saying, '*Aabajitoonan, aabajitoonan*'—Use them, use them." Peter Kelley looked down at his hands. "Two of the women in our settlement were already sewing Ma's burial clothes when we bound the leaves on her swollen leg that night as Amik's grandmother had told us to do. But not a one of us expected those leaves would change a thing, certainly we didn't."

Mr. Kelley stopped and took a long sip of tea.

"And the leaves did?" I asked, hardly daring to believe that they would. It made me shiver to think about that blackened, swelled-up leg with Indian leaves wrapped around it, and the women sewing burial clothes in the next room.

Peter Kelley nodded and gave a wide grin. "In the morning, my Ma was well enough to get out of bed and try on those burial clothes for size."

"Surely not," Laura cried.

"Yes, she was fine and well again," he insisted.

"The leaves did all that?" I said.

Mr. Kelley shrugged. "All I can say is that those of us who saw it with our own eyes believed it to be so. And Ma has lived more than a dozen good years since."

In the silence after he finished his story, I thought about my own Ma. I imagined the old Indian woman with the rabbit bone necklace coming to our cabin when my Ma was dying. Even then, I was certain she never would have taken help from an Indian.

Knowing my Ma, she would rather have died and gone on to the next world than to have allowed Indians to save her. I glanced over at Laura and wondered what we would do if we were in the same place.

Seemed like we were all lost in our thoughts until Mr. Kelley said he didn't mean to keep us from eating our pie, and Laura jumped up to serve the forgotten pieces. I could tell that Mr. Kelley liked that pie real well because he didn't stop to take one breath while eating it. He even picked up the crumbs one by one with the back of his fork. When he finished, he shook his head slowly and said that our Ma's custard pie was the best he'd ever tasted.

Laura just nodded and said that our Ma always was a good cook, but there was still much to be learnt since she had gone.

"Yes, I expect there is," Mr. Kelley said in a quiet way, and I caught him giving Laura a kind look as he pushed back his chair to leave.

When he reached down to pick up the snowshoe, I couldn't help noticing it again. I think he must have seen me staring at it, because he tucked it quickly under his arm and didn't say one word of explanation about it.

All Peter Kelley told us before he left was that he hoped to return one last time before the trial to talk to Amik. Maybe his eyes said that he hoped to see Laura again, too. It was hard telling. But before he disappeared down the path, he turned and waved at us. I remember how he stopped right in the middle of his ambling walk and turned around. Taking off his hat, he waved it once in the air. The sunlight caught his copper red hair, and I had to admit that maybe he was handsome in a skinny sort of way.

That would be the last glimpse we would have of him for nearly two weeks.

*Red Hair says
he will be gone
many nights,
until the end of the flowering moon
is near,
preparing
for the trial.*

*before he leaves
he reaches
deep
inside his coat
to find
a duckbill of sweet maple sugar, and
two acorn cakes
from Rice Bird, and
a bag of tobacco
from Ajijaak, my father.*

*i take the gifts
and Red Hair says—
your wife and children and the Old Ones
wish me to tell you
that their hearts
melt
and they pray to Kitche Manitou
for your return.*

after the trial,
i will go back? i ask.
eɣa',
yes, Red Hair says.

i will hunt in the woods
and fish in the rivers
and see the sun rise
and fall
in the sky again?
eɣa', eɣa', eɣa',
yes, yes, yes, he says.

after Red Hair has gone,
i pour
the sandy grains
of maple sugar
into my mouth.
the taste of the trees
is sweet
on my tongue.

Sixteen

As Indian John's trial drew closer, a gnawing dread began to grow inside me.

It was the same feeling I had at certain other times of the year. I always dreaded the start of the bitter month of March, which had taken Ma away. And the approach of Independence Day on account of how Pa and the men got rolling drunk on whiskey and went wild with their guns. And hog-butchering time because Pa said I was too softhearted.

And now, as the end of May approached, an uneasy feeling had come over me about the trial and what was going to happen. Everywhere I went, it seemed I heard folks talking about Mr. Kelley and Indian John. And most of what they were saying was mean and ugly.

Our gossiping neighbor, Mrs. Evans, said that she

had seen Peter Kelley riding through the settlement. "Yesterday, I think I saw that Indian lawyer," she told us one morning while she was visiting our house. "He was riding an old, swaybacked horse along Water Street. What a poor stick he is." She rolled her eyes. "Looks as if he's never done an ounce of work in his life. They say he don't own no farmland at all, not even a cornfield, 'magine that." She leaned forward and grinned with her poor-looking teeth. "He ain't gonna last one day out here on the frontier, not one day."

I didn't dare to turn my eyes in Laura's direction. The whole time Mrs. Evans was talking, I just stared at the knotholes in our table.

A few days later, I was standing in Mr. Perry's dusty little store buying one stick cinnamon and some sugar when I overheard words that were even worse. Mr. Perry was talking to a stranger. Only thing I could see of the two of them was the tops of their heads over a stack of barrels—Mr. Perry's gray, uncombed hair and the stranger's brown work hat. Mr. Perry was telling the man that there was gonna be a big Indian trial in our settlement in a few days, and after the trial was held, they were gonna hang the savage first and drag the Indian lawyer out of the state on the back of his heels second.

My stomach curled up inside me, and I didn't breathe a word as they spoke to each other. No one knew that me and Laura had gotten to know Mr. Kelley and Indian John. Or that we'd come to feel a great deal of pity in our hearts for them.

"Nay, I wouldn't do that," the stranger replied in a slow voice. "If it was me, I'd give that skinny lawyer a hatchet in the skull, same as that savage done to that poor white trapper. Then I'd throw his bones in the ground and let him go and defend all the misrable savages he wants in hell."

I feared I was going to vomit up everything inside me.

Leaving the stick cinnamon exactly where it was and forgetting my little basket on a barrel, I told Mr. Perry that I was feeling an attack of the shaking ague coming on and I had to get home before I felt any worse. I ran all the way back to the cabin, holding my arms against my stomach and blinking tears out of my eyes.

I couldn't understand how they could speak so cruelly against kind and gentle Peter Kelley, who was only trying to do what he thought was right. Who else would have defended Indian John if he hadn't stepped forward? Wasn't there a single soul who was taking Indian John's side?

I tried asking Amos what he thought. One evening while he was cutting kindling, I stood by the chopping stump, rolling the strings of my apron around and around my finger.

"You want something, Reb?" Amos said finally, giving me a half grin. "Or are you just standing there to see what work looks like?"

"I'm wondering something," I said.

"Wondering ain't getting anything useful done."

"I'm wondering about the Indian's trial."

Amos stopped chopping and wiped his sleeve across his forehead. "What about it?"

"I'm wondering why they're going to the trouble

of a trial and a jury and lawyers if everybody already believes he's guilty."

Amos went back to chopping. "Because that's the way justice is," he said, over the sound of the ax. "If you was a man, you would see that. Even a guilty Indian gets a trial in this country before he gets hanged. That's the fair way things get done."

"But what if—" I paused and took a deep breath. "What if it comes out in the trial that maybe he ain't guilty?"

Amos sighed loudly. "Why don't you ever use your head, Reb? If he wasn't guilty, there wouldn't be a trial, now would there? There wouldn't be no need for a jury or lawyers if he was innocent, right? What kind of sense would that make?" He picked up the ax and lowered it hard, sending splinters of wood everywhere. "Now just go on and leave me alone."

What Amos meant was a bafflement to me. My mind twisted and turned trying to understand his words. They didn't make an ounce of sense, truly they didn't. No matter which way I looked at them.

When I saw Mr. Kelley again, I decided I would ask him what he believed and I would warn him about Mr. Perry and the other men. Even if, like Amos, he thought I was nothing but a rattle-brained fool.

Seventeen

Peter Kelley finally came back on a day that Laura was making soap at the Hawleys'. When I opened the door and saw his familiar coat, I knew that Laura would never forgive herself for leaving. We had just about given up all hope of seeing him again. Day af–ter day, we had jumped at each knock on the door, only to find another person waiting outside.

"May I come in?" Mr. Kelley said in a hurried voice. He had a square haversack slung over one shoulder, and in his left hand, he held a brown leather book that was stuck full of papers.

I nodded and wished that Laura was there. Mercy was playing with a big pile of wood shavings on the floor behind me, and I am sure that I looked like the foolishest thing, with wood shavings stuck all over my clothes. All the things I had been intending to ask Peter Kelley had suddenly left my head.

"Laura ain't here," I said as he stepped inside. "She's gone off to the Hawleys' for the day."

Mr. Kelley hesitated. I watched as he gazed up at the loft above our heads and then back at the door he had come through. I could tell he was considering whether to leave or stay.

"I don't know when I can find a way to return, not with all the men in the fields and the settlement as busy as it is," he mumbled, as if he was speaking to himself more than me. He gave me an uncertain look. "You'll keep an ear out for your Pa and brothers?" he asked.

I nodded.

"You'll tell me if you hear anyone coming down the road?"

I nodded again.

Reluctantly, he started up the steps to the chamber loft. While he was talking to Indian John, I sat in the open doorway of the cabin, slowly cutting up a bowl of potatoes and keeping an eye out for Pa and the boys, who had gone to the settlement. Mercy played on the floor behind me.

I tried to decide what to say to Mr. Kelley before he left. Should I warn him about Mr. Perry and the other men? Tell him everything I had overheard in the store? Was it blasphemous to repeat the words my brother Amos had said about the trial? Or should I just keep silent, as my Pa always said I ought to do?

At the sound of Mr. Kelley's footsteps, my heart

thudded in my chest and my mouth felt dry as ashes. I could not think of what words to say. The questions tossed to and fro in my mind. He would surely think I was a half-wit or a fool if I spoke. And how could I go against my Pa and the men?

I ran my tongue across my lips. As Mr. Kelley was tucking the brown book back into his haversack, I stammered quickly, "Will you win, do you think?" It was not the question I was fixing to ask, but it was the only one that came out.

"Win?" He squinted at me.

"The trial," I said.

Peter Kelley's forehead wrinkled up as if he was thinking what to say, and his serious brown eyes stared at me for what seemed like a long time before he replied. I reckon maybe he didn't want to answer on account of who my Pa was and what I might tell him.

But finally, he said, "Yes, Miss Rebecca. I will win."

His voice was as sure and solid as a block of stone, and I had to swallow hard when I heard it because I figured he didn't know a thing about Mr. Perry and the men.

"What if the men aim—" I paused, praying that Pa would never find out what I did. "What if the men aim, well, to cause you trouble?" I said in a voice that was almost a whisper.

"Trouble?"

"At the trial," I mumbled. "Because of you, well, defending an Indian."

Mr. Kelley slung his haversack over his shoulder and gave me a wide easy grin. "I don't expect the judge or the sheriff would stand for that," he said with a shrug. "And if someone didn't serve as the lawyer for the Indian's side, what sort of trial would there be?"

Peter Kelley ducked through the doorway and was gone before I could tell him what my brother had said. Or that, truth be told, the sheriff for the Crooked River settlement might not help him either. He was one of my Pa's good friends. And he was none too fond of Indians either, from what I knew.

But perhaps Peter Kelley was right. Perhaps the judge would be on his side.

in my mind
i hear the words
of Red Hair
telling me how it will be.

when I am brought
to the trial,
i will stand before a judge
and twelve other white men
who will decide
right and wrong.

i do not understand
i tell my old friend.

if an Indian murders a man,
it is the man's family—
brothers, sons, fathers—
who decide
right and wrong.
they are the only ones who know
what should be done.

why would a white chief
and twelve strangers
take revenge for a murder
that has not happened to them?
i ask.

Red Hair says it is the law
of the white men—
they must prove
that i am guilty of the crime.

but i am not guilty,
i tell Red Hair,
and if they asked the family
of the murdered man
they would know
i speak the truth.

my friend sighs and tells me
that after i see it
with my own eyes
and listen
with my own ears,
i will understand
the fair justice
of the white man.

Eighteen

June 1812

The judge arrived a few days before the trial was set to begin.

It was the first week of June when he came riding into our settlement. The weather had been warm and dry, and the corn had been in the ground for a good while. The beets and potatoes were already coming up in the garden, and we had more onions than we cared to eat.

Our gossiping neighbor Mrs. Evans was the one who came barreling down the path to our house to tell us the judge had arrived.

Hammering her big knuckles on the door frame to get our attention, Mrs. Evans gasped, out of breath,

"That judge we been waiting for is here. My husband seen him with his own eyes."

If you ranked men in order of importance, the most important man to meet would likely be the president, next the governor, and right after that would be the traveling judges who came for the court days.

Since none of us had a prayer of ever meeting President Madison and not likely Governor Meigs either, everyone was always anxious to get a glimpse of the judges when they passed through our settlement like minor kings. They always had fine-cut frock coats from the city, handsome riding horses, and a collection of mysterious leather bags and round portmanteaus tied to their saddles.

"It's Judge James Randolph Noble," Mrs. Evans continued. "That's what my husband said."

Judge James Randolph Noble.

I don't know why, but hearing his fancy name gave me some hope. I pictured the judge in his flowing black robes, looking like Moses giving out the Ten Commandments. A judge named James Randolph Noble would see to it that justice was done for Peter Kelley and Indian John, surely he would.

Mrs. Evans, who was an everlasting talker, said the courtroom for the judge was being set up under the big shady tree next to Mr. Perry's store. "Anybody who can fill up a foot of space and put the fear of God in that wretched savage is invited to come and hear it, they says—even women and children and babes in arms," Mrs. Evans rattled on.

Mrs. Evans peered at us. "I reckon both of you is gonna be there with your Pa and brothers, ain't you?"

When me and Laura didn't answer, Mrs. Evans leaned forward, eyeing us more closely. "Now you ain't just gonna stay here in your old house, are you? Don't you want to see that Indian get his comeuppance for what he done? Setting here by yourselves won't be half as good as watching all that."

She shook her finger at Laura. "You just tell that Pa of yours to let you come and watch. I don't see why Major Carver would find fault with letting his girls come to a savage's trial. You tell him Mrs. Evans will keep an eye on you. Just tell him that." She turned to leave. "And I'm gonna borrow one of your milk buckets while I'm here, too, if you don't mind."

And without waiting to hear a word from us, she headed out the door in the direction of our barn and was gone.

After Mrs. Evans left, Laura heaved a deep sigh. "I don't care to go to that trial at all," she said. "Let everybody leave us to ourselves. You and me, we'll take a pinch or two of loaf sugar and make some fancy little cakes in the reflector oven. Like the ones Ma used to have for company. And we'll put on our good bonnets and find a place to sit near the cabin, and we'll drink green tea and eat our fancy little cakes. Let Pa and the men do what they will."

To tell the honest truth, I didn't want to see the trial either. I knew what Peter Kelley had told me—how he was going to win. And I knew what my Pa and the settlement all believed. And I knew that Judge James R. Noble was there to see that fair justice was done. Looking at it from all of these directions, I believed that nothing good could possibly come out of the trial for anyone.

But Pa wouldn't hear of us staying home.

"Carvers is gonna be at the trial," he said when Laura tried to reason with him at supper that night. She told him that we were planning to do some baking and keep an eye on Mercy rather than going to watch the trial proceedings.

"You just bring Mercy along with you and make her mind," he said in a hard voice. "And you make your bread and such some other day. All of us is gonna be at the trial."

the gichi-mookomaanag
paint my face
in crooked stripes.
they take me
from the place
that floats above the ground.

outside

i lift up my head
and smell the corn
growing in the fields
and the fish
swimming in the rivers
and the wild red berries
turning full and ripe
in the woods.

i hear the deer moving
with their fawns
and the snapping turtles
coming up from the rivers
and the rattlesnakes curled
asleep
in the sunlight.

i believe
the gichi-mookomaanag
are blind and deaf—

they do not turn their heads
to look up at the sky.
they do not hear the sound
of their loud feet.

they pull me
through the woods
at the end of their iron rope,
talking of death
in words they think i do not know.

they see and hear
nothing
that lives.

Nineteen

On the day of the trial, we didn't leave until the sun was nearly above the tops of the trees, long after Pa and my brothers had left. It seemed as if we had been awake for hours. Days, even. I had tossed and turned all night, fearing what would happen. Laura looked worn to shadows, too.

It had been awful hard listening to Pa and the men getting Indian John ready in the morning. I don't think me or Laura ever imagined they would use the soot from our own kettles and fat from the grease pot to paint stripes on Indian John's face. By the time they left with Indian John, both our stomachs were turned. Only Mercy had an appetite for her breakfast, while me and Laura didn't eat much more than a mouthful of ours.

We washed the breakfast dishes in silence. I

scrubbed the plates in small circles while Laura dried them just as slow. After the dishes were done, we took our time combing our hair, and I mended a torn hem in Laura's good dress. Twice.

Finally, when there wasn't any more time to be wasted—and we knew Pa would be looking for us—we pulled on our bonnets and tucked our hair carefully inside. Before we closed the cabin door, Laura took a pinch of camphor from one of our tins and put it in her workbag. The sight of her bringing that along filled me with dread. Camphor was for funerals and sitting up with somebody's remains. It brought you back to your senses if you were overcome. I asked Laura why she would take it to the trial, and she said there was no telling what we would see that day, no telling at all.

Holding tight to Mercy's little hands, we made our way down the road toward the settlement. White gnats flew in clouds around us and we had to keep a sharp eye for snakes curled up on the warm dirt. "Where we going?" Mercy kept on asking, and Laura kept on answering, "Hush."

As we drew closer to the settlement, I figured we would surely hear the trial.

But we didn't hear a word until we came out of the woods and saw the silent crowd of spectators gathered around Mr. Perry's store. I had never seen so many people in one place in all my life. Not for In-dependence Day or a cabin raising or a funeral either. They didn't fit in the shade of the big tree but spilled out in every direction.

"Lord, look at the people," Laura gasped. "Reb, look at all the people."

The crowd sat on all manner of things—wagon boxes, planks, upended logs, and fancy chairs. Whatever they could find or bring, I supposed. Around the edges, there were bed quilts and blankets scattered across the scraggled grass, filled with women and children.

As me and Laura drew closer, we caught sight of the jury men. They sat on two rows of planks near the front of the crowd. There were twelve of them, and I noticed a few faces I knew among them—our neighbor Mr. Evans, the shoemaker Hiram Nash, old Vinegar Bigger, the rough Hoadley brothers, who were rumored to be overly fond of drinking whiskey slings, Mr. Hawley—and a half dozen others. Most of the men looked mighty uncomfortable in their good suits of clothes, with their faces still sunburnt from planting. I could see their pocket handkerchiefs moving up to wipe their foreheads.

Judge James R. Noble was next to the jury. He sat behind a table that was placed on a raised box.

I studied him. He wasn't exactly like the picture I had drawn in my mind. I had imagined someone tall and white-haired. Someone who would make everyone take notice and tremble. But Judge Noble was a round and fleshy-faced sort of man. His brown hair had retreated far back, leaving a wide white forehead that caught the shine of the sun. And his black robes hung in loose folds around him.

When we reached the edge of the crowd, the judge was talking to someone sitting on the right side of him in what seemed to be the witness chair.

The man was dressed in a dark suit of clothes, and he had a good brown hat resting in his lap.

It gave me a start to realize that the man sitting there, being spoken to by the judge himself, was my very own Pa.

Twenty

Mrs. Evans caught sight of us and waved us over to a row where she was sitting. "Your Pa's up there testifying to the truth right now," she hollered out, loud as an old crow, and my cheeks flushed when people's heads turned to stare.

As we sat down next to Mrs. Evans, we heard the judge say that the jury would now hear the testimony of the witness, Major Lorenzo Carver.

I saw Augustus Root stand up and move toward my Pa. He was a lawyer from the East who had been living in our settlement for nearly two years. But I must confess, me and Laura never took much of a liking to him. Mr. Root seemed to think more highly of himself than a person should and was terribly fond of listening to the sound of his own voice.

He was also the only man we knew who still

dressed in knee breeches and stockings. And truth to speak, Mr. Root's legs were nothing to look at neither. Scrawny old bird legs in white stockings. When no one was around, me and Laura called him Rooster Root on account of his legs and his peculiar habit of puffing out his chest when he spoke.

"Tell us, Major Carver," he said, moving in quick steps toward the witness chair. "Tell us in your own words exactly what happened in regards to the Indian we have brought before us this morning."

"Well, now." My Pa gazed at Mr. Root and answered slowly. "I think you and everybody else on the jury knows exactly what happened. I don't need to go and repeat all the details, do I, Augustus?" He looked out at the crowd. "We all live 'round here and we ain't the kinds to keep secrets, is we?"

But I could tell that the judge was none too pleased with this answer. His shoulders rose up so his robe was almost touching his ears, and he leaned forward to stare at my Pa in the witness chair.

"Mr. Carver," he said slowly, giving my Pa a look that could have withered a cornstalk in July. "I don't give one damned fig what everybody in this town knows or doesn't know. This is a court of law. You tell the jury exactly what you know. Do you understand?"

Right at that moment, I felt a small flicker of hope for Indian John and Peter Kelley. I didn't dare to look over at Laura, but I could hear her give a soft whisper under her breath. Maybe Peter Kelley was right about the judge being more powerful than any of the men in our settlement. I had never seen anybody stand up to my Pa. He was feared on both sides of the river. But Judge James R. Noble didn't seem to take any notice of that fact.

In the silence after the judge scolded my Pa, I watched as Mr. Root patted a handkerchief carefully across his forehead and blew his nose loudly. I figured my father was supposed to be on the same side as him, and my Pa was not acting according to his plans. But then he didn't act according to anyone's plans except his own.

Mr. Root took a long while to fold his handkerchief into a small, neat square and tuck it back in his frock coat before beginning again. I guessed he was trying to give Pa time to stop stewing in his chair.

"To continue," he said finally, giving Pa a small, encouraging smile. "Please tell us, Major Carver, in your own words, what happened earlier this spring and how you came to capture the Indian before us today."

My Pa crossed his arms and leaned back in his chair. He fixed his eyes on Mr. Root and didn't look once at the crowd or the jury and especially not the judge. Just spoke straight to the lawyer, as if he was the only other person there.

"In the month of April, this year," he said, "me and my men got word that a poor trapper named Gibbs had been found dead—kilt by Indians at the end of March."

"And where was the trapper found?"

"Other side of Crooked River." Pa waved his arm as if he was standing right on the river's edge. "Over there, the western side."

"And what did you do after hearing about the dead trapper?"

"Well," Pa said, sending a hard spit of tobacco to the ground. "I got all my men together, maybe ten of us there was, and we went 'cross the river at the end of April to hunt for the three Indians who done it."

"I see." Mr. Root nodded slowly and rubbed his chin, as if he was pretending to think hard. "You say Indians did this," he repeated. "But how did you know that for certainty, Major Carver?"

"Whether or not Indians kilt the trapper, you mean?"

"Yes." Mr. Root nodded solemnly.

Pa gave a little snort. "He had an Indian toma-hawk stuck into his skull, that's how." He paused and added, "Reckon that would kill jist about anybody, now wouldn't it?"

A wave of laughter rippled through the crowd and the judge leaned forward to say something. But before he did, Mr. Root hurried on with his next question.

"How did you know which particular Indians did it?"

"Folks around here and over there told us," Pa said. "They ain't dumb."

"What folks?"

"Do I gotta go and name them all?" Pa scowled. "I ain't got all year to set here for this trial."

"Just a few of them," Mr. Root insisted, taking out his folded handkerchief again. "If you wouldn't mind, Mr. Carver, please."

"I'll see if I can recollect them all," Pa answered

with a loud sigh. "We talked to blacksmith Nichols, who made the Indian's tomahawk...the man who found the fellow dead on his land...'nother trapper who hunted with the dead man...a fellow whose barn got burnt down by the same Indians last summer...," he said, counting them one by one on his fingers as if to show how many there were.

"And all of them told you the same thing?"

"Yes sir."

"What was it that they told you, exactly?"

"That the murder had been done by three particular Indians who had been giving them trouble for a while."

"Three Indians," Mr. Root repeated loudly.

My Pa nodded. "One of which"—he pointed—"is sitting over there."

The crowd hushed as everybody leaned forward to look in the direction of Indian John, who was seated in a chair near the front. I was pleased that his chair didn't face the crowd. All anybody could get a glimpse of was the back of his head and the brown cloth of his plain shirt. The white blanket that I had often seen folded next to him in the loft was draped over his left shoulder. Only the judge and jury could see the fierce stripes that my Pa made.

"When you say 'trouble,' of what sort do you mean?" continued Mr. Root.

Pa leaned forward and put his hands on his knees. "Augustus, you know as well as me that we have been bothered by these hostile, savage Indians for years. I don't got to name all the troubles they cause." He spit loudly and wiped his mouth with the back of his hand. "We try to clear our land, plant our fields, raise our families in peace, and they kill our women and children, steal our food, burn down our barns. Ain't no secret who's doing it if you live around here."

Folks all around me were nodding and agreeing as if it had happened to every last one of them. To be truthful, I didn't know anybody it had happened to. Nobody in the Crooked River settlement had ever been kilt by Indians. Not in my memory. Only thing I had ever heard were stories from other places.

"Enough," the judge said loudly, pinning a glare on Pa and Augustus Root.

"Thank you, Your Honor," Mr. Root said quickly. "That's all."

There were some hoots and shouts from the men in the crowd, but I couldn't tell the meaning exactly. Regardless, the judge didn't appear to pay them any mind. He just turned toward the other side of his table. "Your questions, Mr. Kelley."

As Mr. Kelley stood up and walked toward the witness stand, it seemed that a dark cloud was cast over the sun and the air got suddenly colder. Folks leaned back and crossed their arms as if they had caught a chill. I heard a loud whispering start up all around me. Maybe the judge heard it, too, because he gave the crowd a long, sweeping stare.

"Mr. Kelley," he repeated loudly. "According to the law, it is now your turn to question the witness, Major Carver—as he is popularly known."

My heart pounded as young Mr. Kelley walked slowly toward my Pa's chair.

One time, we had a little brown dog who was kilt one morning trying to fight off a wild bear. If you have ever seen that happen, you know the sickening feeling that comes from watching the terrible scene unfold and being helpless to do a thing about it. That's exactly how I felt as Mr. Kelley stood in front of my Pa.

"Mr.—Major Carver," Peter Kelley said, in a voice that was full of nerves. "You say you were told—or, well, heard—that three Indians were responsible for this crime, correct?"

"Yessir," my Pa shot back. "That's what I said."

"So, you didn't see the dead man yourself?"

My Pa leaned forward ominously, and just out of pure habit, I moved back in my seat. "You trying to tell me that the poor trapper weren't dead?" he said real low.

Peter Kelley's face turned a shade of red, and he stumbled over his answer. "I'm only trying to find out what you saw so the jury knows exactly—"

"I don't need to see a dead man to know he's dead," my Pa spat.

From behind them came the judge's voice. "Answer the question, Mr. Carver. Did you see the dead man with your own eyes?"

"No."

"The witness says no," the judge repeated, giving Peter Kelley a stern, fatherly sort of look. "Move on to your next question."

I could see the lawyer's shoulders go up and down as he took in a trembling breath of air. He shuffled through the papers in his hand, and when he started up again, it seemed to me that he spoke with a trifle more courage and conviction.

"Would you describe the three Indians you tried to catch?"

"There was two grown Indians and one real young boy, maybe seven or eight years of age."

"And what happened to them?"

"Well, the boy run off from us before we could catch him. We were told by that Indian"—Pa motioned toward Indian John—"that the boy was known by the name of Semo."

when I hear the name Semo,
i laugh
inside my mouth.

the men who caught me
wanted the name
of the young Indian
who ran.
i told them
Se Mo.
shame and dirt.

the gichi-mookomaanag
wandered in the woods
for hours
calling out
shame and
dirt. shame
and dirt.

while my son
Little Otter,
slipped away.

inside my mouth,
i laugh.

Twenty-one

"Pardon me?" Mr. Kelley said, and I saw his eyes dart over to Indian John.

"I said SE–MO," Pa spat. "You listenin' or not?"

There was a peculiar silence before Peter Kelley continued. His eyes flickered in the direction of Indian John again and then he coughed a little and returned to his questions. "And what do you remember about the other two Indians?" he said.

"The other Indian was older. He run off before we caught him and shot himself with his own gun."

Mr. Kelley squinted at Pa, as if he was pretending to be confused. "While he was running, you say? He shot and killed himself with his own gun?" You could tell by the way his voice rose that he didn't believe a word my Pa said.

Mr. Root leaped up to shout an objection and the

judge leaned across the table. "Mr. Kelley," he said slowly, as if speaking to a child. "This is a case about a dead trapper, not a dead Indian, am I correct?"

Mr. Kelley nodded and repeated his apologies twice. Around us, everyone seemed impatient to move and the children in the back were fussing loudly. A man in the crowd stood up and hollered something about Mr. Kelley that doesn't bear repeating. It was already well past the noon mealtime.

"Have your questions for this witness been concluded, Mr. Kelley?" The judge sighed.

"Yes sir, that was all, I think, yes," Mr. Kelley said. Even though from the downcast look on his face, I don't imagine that they were.

Standing up and wiping a cloth across his shiny bald head, the judge told everyone that the next witness would have to wait until the court had some refreshments and its noonday meal. Although I daresay from the weary expressions on the faces of the judge and jury, none of them were very anxious to return to the Indian's trial again.

As we walked back to the cabin, Mrs. Evans huffed, "That miserable lawyer has nothing but lies in his mouth. Just full of outright lies. I don't see how he can stand up there and say those things to your Pa."

I didn't breathe a word, but while we walked, I kept on wondering about Mr. Kelley's question. How could a man be running and shoot himself with his own gun?

the words of the white men
roll with lies.

Ten Claws
has the legs
of an old man,
of a slow crane bird,
of a turtle.

i hear the snap
of the white man's gun,
but i do not feel
its sting. beside me
Ten Claws
is the one who cries and
falls.

Ten Claws
has the legs
of an old man,
of a slow crane bird,
of a turtle,
but even Ten Claws
does not run
slow enough
to shoot
himself
with his own gun.

Twenty-two

When the court resumed again in the late afternoon, a large bear of a man filled the entire witness chair. I drew in my breath.

Blacksmith Nichols.

In the settlement, the sight of him always frightened me near to death. His soot black hands were the size of bear paws. Beneath his rolled-up sleeves, his red arms were as big around as tree limbs. But it was his fierce eyes that truly seemed to burn holes straight through your skin if you caused him to turn them in your direction. Whenever he came to visit my Pa, I sat in terror of him.

But Augustus Root didn't seem to feel even a shiver of fear. After the blacksmith was sworn to tell the truth, he strolled easily toward him. "Tell us, if you would, Mr. Nichols," he started, in a voice that was almost cheerful, as if he was asking Mr. Nichols to tea. "How did you come to make the acquaintance of the Indian who is before us today, the one who is called—"

"Made him a tomahawk," the blacksmith's voice rumbled, and he stuck his finger in Indian John's direction before Mr. Root even finished all his words.

"A tomahawk," Mr. Root repeated slowly.

"Yes sir."

"And why did you make a tomahawk for this particular Indian?"

Mr. Nichols crossed his arms and glared at the lawyer. "You seen many blacksmiths among the savages, Mr. Root?"

Not a soul in the crowd dared to laugh.

Augustus Root smiled uncomfortably. "No, of course not, quite so." He straightened the fancy white cloth tied around his neck and smoothed the front of his yellow silk vest before speaking again. I hid a small grin behind my hand.

"Could you, perhaps, describe the tomahawk you made for Indian John?" he said, gesturing with one arm. "Tell the jury, well, exactly how it was made."

Mr. Nichols stared at the lawyer as if he had asked an even more thick-skulled question. "What a tomahawk is *made* of?" he repeated.

"Let me remind everyone," the judge interrupted, "that this is a court of law and all questions are to be answered to the best of one's knowledge."

Seemed to me that the blacksmith grew even larger as he drew back his anvil-sized shoulders and turned his fierce eyes upon the judge.

"Mr. Nichols, could you explain how the tomahawk was made exactly? Just for the jury," the lawyer hurried on.

There was a long terrifying wait before Nichols turned toward the crowd again and answered the lawyer.

"It was a pipe tomahawk. Iron blade with a steel edge. For sharpness," he added in a voice that sent a chill clear through my bones.

"And you made only the blade, am I correct?"

"Yes."

"What about the haft—the handle? What did it look like?"

"Wood."

"Any decoration that you recall?"

"Yes."

Augustus Root stopped and rubbed his eyes, as if he was growing weary of asking question after question without getting anything more than a yes or no. "Could you perhaps describe it?" he said, sighing loudly.

"There was marks scorched all along the wood of the haft." Mr. Nichols moved his hands. "Dark and light stripes."

"Made by the Indian?"

"Made by some Indian," the blacksmith rumbled. "I don't know who."

"Anything else? Other decorations?"

"One piece of trade silver in the shape of a diamond, set in the wood."

The lawyer glanced out at the crowd and said in a louder voice, as if he wanted all of us to hear him.

"Do you think, Mr. Nichols, you would recognize the tomahawk you worked on if it was shown to you again?"

My heart thudded in my chest.

"Yes," Mr. Nichols said, folding his big arms. "I would."

Grinning a little to himself, Augustus Root walked quickly to his chair to fetch something. In an anxious rush of air, everyone around us stood up to see it.

i have seen the tomahawk
of Ten Claws
many times.

he wore it
proudly
tucked in the woven red sash
tied around his waist.

it is handsome—
as the gichi-mookomaan
holds it overhead,
i see
the flash of silver
and the handle
half as long as a man's arm,
circled
with bands of black
and brown
like a striped insect
that hums over summer fields.

but i know, too,
that the tomahawk
of Ten Claws
flies on angry wings
when it is thrown.

i remember
how Ten Claws was too much mad,
how he took his tomahawk one night
and plunged into the dark and snow.
we called out to him,
béka! béka! stop!
but he would listen to
no one.

Twenty-three

I knew by the whispering sound of the crowd that the tomahawk was exactly the one the blacksmith had described. Exactly the one he had made for Indian John. And the same one that had been found in the trapper's head. Stinging tears began to fill my eyes and a lump rose fast in my throat.

"Is this the pipe tomahawk you recollect making?" I heard Augustus Root say loudly, and the blacksmith did not take more than a half second to examine it before I heard him answer that it was.

"Could you show us the person you made it for?" the lawyer continued.

The blacksmith stood up and pointed his finger.

My heart sank to my feet.

"That Indian is who I made it for. That one sitting right there," he said, in a voice that was sure as anything.

Some in the crowd wanted to see Indian John hanged without hearing another word. A man with a face full of pox scars waved his arm at the judge and hollered out, "You heared what that Nichols fellow said. Jist hang the savage from this big tree right here and be done with it."

I looked up at the wide oak tree above us and held my arms across my sickening stomach.

"Silence!"

As the crowd clapped and cheered, Judge James R. Noble pounded his mallet so hard on his table, I expect it probably made circles in the wood. "I am the judge of this state of Ohio," he bellowed when the crowd grew quiet. "And I don't give a pickled damn who you want to hang or when." He leaned across the table, his face as red as clay bricks, and stared furiously at everyone. "You will not—by the laws of the United States or the ones written by God himself—hang anyone until I give the word that justice is done."

The judge gestured toward poor Mr. Kelley and said that he had every right to take his turn, even if the Indian was as guilty as a fox in a henhouse. "Every right," he repeated, and glared at the crowd.

But I could tell that there wasn't enough time left for Mr. Kelley to question the blacksmith. In the nearby fields, the cows were beginning to bellow for their milking, and there was a day's worth of chores still left to do. So, the judge said the trial would conclude for the day and resume the next morning.

The crowd grumbled as they began to pick up their sundry collection of chairs and benches. "Ain't nothing left to try," I could hear people saying to each other. "Guilty as guilty is," they mumbled. "Waste our time listening to nothing. Jist hang him."

Me and Laura kept our heads down as we walked back to the cabin with Mercy. I felt plain shaken inside. I didn't know what to think. In my mind, I tried to reason that perhaps Mr. Nichols was mistaken. Or that the trapper had been kilt by another tomahawk, exactly like the one the blacksmith had made. But Mr. Nichols was the only blacksmith we had, and who would recognize a tomahawk better than him?

Laura looked over at me. "You feeling as dreadful bad as I am?"

I nodded.

"I just feel so sorry for Peter Kelley." Laura's voice wavered. "I think he must have believed every word Indian John told him. They were friends, and so he thought..." Her voice trailed away.

"Yes," I said low, scuffing my feet along the hard wagon ruts of the road.

"What will Mr. Kelley say tomorrow?" she whispered. "Or do?"

I couldn't imagine what Mr. Kelley would do the next day or how he would prove the blacksmith wrong. But the rest of the evening, my mind kept repeating the words he had said to me. *I will win.*

Even though it didn't seem likely that Mr. Nichols would be mistaken in front of God and all those men, I could not give up on those words. No matter what everybody else, even Laura, thought to be true, my mind still held on to *I will win.*

Twenty-four

The next morning, the sky poured rain. When I heard it on the roof as I was lying in bed, I nearly shouted for joy. There wouldn't be any trial beneath Mr. Perry's old tree. Not in the hard rain. But then Pa came stomping in while we were fixing breakfast and told us the trial would be held inside our cabin on account of the poor weather and because our log house was the biggest one.

I couldn't keep a downcast look from crossing my face. Pa caught a glimpse of it and said he had best not ever see that look again—hard work was what we did, and if I didn't want a thrashing, I had better help Laura get everything in order. I didn't dare to tell him that it wasn't the work I didn't want to do.

After Pa left, I took some breakfast up to Indian John. He was sitting with his knees drawn up to his chest and his arms wrapped around them, staring into the shadows as if he was thinking. I don't know if he understood what all the shuffling and noise meant below, but he didn't nod in my direction as he usually did.

As I set down the plate of food, I noticed that his white blanket was crumpled in the middle of the loft floor. I figured that it had fallen off his shoulders while the men were putting him back in irons and no one had cared to pick it up. Someone ought to show Amik one small kindness, I thought. No matter what happened at the miserable trial that day.

So, I lifted up the white blanket from where it lay in a heap, shook the dust out of it, and folded it as neatly as one of our own bed quilts. Before I went back down the steps, I put the blanket beside his straw pallet and smoothed it with my hands. The blanket was wool with a band of red along the side, and I imagine it was important to him. It would have been important to me, anyway.

I didn't say a word to Laura about it when I came downstairs. With people already arriving, we had to hurry to move all our furnishings and such to the walls. By midmorning, folks were packed into our cabin so tightly that not a chink of air remained. They were crowded on our beds, and Lorenzo even perched on top of our flour barrel.

Me and Laura settled in the farthest corner of the room, behind all of the water-soaked backs and heads. We sat on the top of our wooden chest so no other folks would use it as their seat. It made my heart pound to imagine what would happen if anybody stumbled upon the things we had hidden inside. What would they think if they opened the wooden cover and caught a glimpse of the beads and quills and such?

From where we sat, we could see Judge Noble, who was placed squarely in front of our fireplace, behind our dinner table. The jury was on the judge's left, crowded on chairs and stools in front of our food cupboard. The lawyers had the other side of the hearth to themselves. They sat in two of our good straight-backed chairs from the East with our dried bunches of herbs dangling strangely above their heads. Indian John sat on the far side of Peter Kelley, nearly hidden in the cabin corner.

The judge hammered his mallet on our table. "Come to order," he called out. I noticed that his hair was wet and unruly from the rain. He kept running his hand over the top of his wide forehead, trying to smooth away the lingering drops of water.

"We are returning to the testimony of blacksmith Nichols this morning," he said, clearing his throat. "And as planned, we will hear the questions of the lawyer Mr. Kelley today."

From the side of the fireplace, Mr. Kelley stood up and walked toward blacksmith Nichols, who was sitting in a chair beside the judge's table. Laura stared down at her fingers, knotting and unknotting them. A lump rose in my throat as I watched Peter Kelley square his thin shoulders and face the blacksmith.

His copper red hair was combed neatly, I noticed, and he wore a vest and shirt that looked newly made, but seeing those things made my heart ache even more. How would it feel to be in his shoes? I wondered. Having to defend the life of a person who was once your friend?

For Mr. Kelley's sake, may something go well, I prayed. Just one small thing.

"Good morning, Mr. Nichols," the lawyer said in a quiet voice. "I only have a few questions." Even those simple words made the crowd mock him in low whispers. Beside me, Laura shook her head.

Mr. Kelley didn't seem to pay the whispers any mind. He held up the striped tomahawk again. "You made this tomahawk for the Indian called Indian John, am I correct?"

Nichols rolled his eyes and gave a sigh loud enough for the whole room to hear. "I already said that to the lawyer yesterday, if you was listening."

"Answer the question Mr. Kelley asked you," the judge warned.

"Yes," the blacksmith's voice rumbled. "Answer ain't no different than yesterday's—yes."

"Thank you," Peter Kelley said, setting the tomahawk on the corner of the judge's table. He walked across the room to fetch something from a sack beside his chair. I raised my head to see what he was doing. He held up a small hatchet with a wood handle, the kind most of the men carried. Not much different than the tomahawk except for its plain handle.

"I'm just curious, Mr. Nichols," Peter Kelley said. "How about this hatchet? Do you recollect making this one?" He handed it to the blacksmith. "Go on— take a closer look at it."

A peculiar expression passed across Nichols's face

as he took that hatchet from Mr. Kelley. He gazed at it for a good long while, turning it over and over in his big hands and running his thumb along the side of the blade, and then he said, "Nope. It ain't one of mine."

"You're certain?" Mr. Kelley repeated. "This isn't the one you made in the fall of last year for Reverend Doan?" Reverend Doan was a Methodist circuit preacher who came through from time to time. I could tell by the way Mr. Kelley asked the question that the hatchet surely belonged to the minister. But I didn't see what Reverend Doan's hatchet had to do with anything.

"I said—it ain't one of mine," Nichols warned.

"This one?" Mr. Kelley held up another plain hatchet, and the blacksmith didn't even look at it. Just kept his eyes on Mr. Kelley's face and said, "It ain't mine."

"How about this one? Certainly you will recognize this one." Mr. Kelley held up another tomahawk. It was striped with scorch marks like Indian John's pipe tomahawk, but it had two silver bands around it and a pewter-looking piece on the end of the handle. "Tell the jury which Indian this belongs to, Mr. Nichols. Certainly you remember."

My heart thudded inside me as I watched Nichols's face grow darker by the minute.

"Perhaps you'll remember the owner of this one—"

As Mr. Kelley reached for another tomahawk, the blacksmith jumped up suddenly and raged, "I ain't answering no more of your questions, you skinny little cuss." The judge stood up and pounded his mallet, but Nichols didn't pay it any mind.

"Maybe I don't know every damn savage I made a tomahawk for," he roared in Mr. Kelley's drawn and fearful face. "But sure as the devil is in hell, I know the one I made for that savage." He pointed at Indian John. "And I dare—DARE—any man in this room to call me a liar to my face," he bellowed. "You go on and have your court of fools—but I'm done answering questions. DONE." He plowed through the crowd of people, pushing a woman and a little toddling child out of his path as he thundered out of our cabin.

After the door closed behind him, the whole room was as still as the woods after a windstorm. The only sound was the rain hammering down on the roof shingles.

"The court calls a rest for an hour," the judge said, breaking the silence. "And we shall discuss how to continue with the testimony—"

I think everyone was startled when Mr. Kelley spoke up.

"No. No," he said, walking toward the judge. "Proceed with the next witness." He waved his hand in the direction of the door. "My questions for the blacksmith were complete. I only wanted to point out"—Mr. Kelley glanced at the jury men—"the outright lies and untruths in Mr. Nichols's testimony about the tomahawk, Your Honor." He said the words "lies and untruths" loud enough and slow enough for everybody in the whole room to hear. The other lawyer jumped up to raise an objection to Peter Kelley's statement, but the judge held up a hand to silence him. "No," he said, impatiently. "We will just proceed…."

As the judge wrote something down, I could hear an angry hum fill the room. It sounded like a nest of bees. I don't think anyone was too pleased with the new direction the trial had suddenly taken. Or with the words "lies and untruths."

In front of us, Mr. Perry swore loudly. "If they find that savage innocent, I'll take up my gun and kill him myself. You jist watch me." Heads nodded all around him.

My mind tossed and turned, trying to understand what I'd heard. Blacksmith Nichols had sworn to tell the truth, the whole truth, hadn't he? I remembered his big hand resting on the judge's Bible and all of his fierce nods and "yes sir's." But I couldn't see how he was able to recollect Indian John's tomahawk clearly and none of the others. And why had Peter Kelley's questions sent him into a wild rage? Was his whole story nothing but lies?

Up in the front of the hearth, the third witness sank down in the chair. He appeared to be about the age of my Pa, but he was more scrawny. One of his thin shoulders stuck up higher than the other, which gave him an odd, crooked appearance.

The judge's voice called for order. "We will now hear the testimony of Mr. Ezra Phelps," he announced. "Mr. Root, you may begin your questions."

i stare at the man
who sits
in the talking chair.
he is well known to me.

five summers ago
he came from a distant place
to fish in our rivers
and hunt in our woodlands
and feed his children
on that which
was not given to him.

when he talks
the crooked
gichi-mookomaan
speaks from three sides
of his mouth
at once.

friend, he calls us.
friend.
but his words roll
like logs in
white water.
didibin, didibin,

didibin,
roll, roll,
roll,
his words
roll with
lies.

Twenty-five

"Mr. Phelps, you and your family live on the other side of the Crooked River, am I right?" Augustus Root said, beginning his questions with a too-wide smile.

The witness bobbed his head in a way that reminded me of eggs in a kettle of boiling water and gave him a polite, yes sir.

"And you have lived there for about five years?"

The witness nodded again. "Got ten acres in corn," he said.

"And you found the dead trapper? Correct?"

"Yes sir," the witness said, sitting up straighter. "Me and my son Asa done found that dead trapper one morning at the edge of one of our cornfields."

"What morning was it?"

Mr. Phelps rolled his eyes upward. "Now, let's see if I can recollect. It was somewhere 'long about the end of March. A Tuesday morning, I believe, be-cause—yes"—he looked at someone in the crowd—"that's right, my wife was washing clothes and she mostly does her washing on Tuesdays."

"Could you describe what you and your son saw?"

"Well, now." Mr. Phelps scratched his cheek and eyed the crowded room nervously. "Judge, I don't want to frighten all them women and children set-ting out there. It weren't a pretty sight what I saw."

The judge sighed. "The observers will bear that in mind. Continue on."

"Well, the body was lying facedown in the snow," the witness said slowly. "The tomahawk was stuck there in its head. Jist like, you know—" The man paused and blinked at the crowd. "Well, I'm real sorry for describing this, but, well, it had cleaved off part of the scalp," he said. "And from what we could see, it done tore out a narrow piece of the poor man's skull—"

I could hear a dozen or more "Lord have mercy's" echo through the cabin. One old woman slipped out the door, holding a handkerchief to her mouth.

Laura reached over and squeezed my hand. "You want to go on outside?" she whispered. I shook my head no, even though I did.

The man paused and spoke louder, as if he was trying to stir things up. "There was a river of dried blood all down the man's back and it had even pooled up in the snow. Me and my son nearly keeled over sick at the sight. Didn't we, Asa?" The witness bobbed his head at his son, who seemed to be sitting in the middle of the crowd.

"Did you know who the murderer was?" Mr. Root asked.

"Yessir, I did, right away." The man's head bobbed up and down again.

"How did you know that?"

"The tomahawk. Once I saw that tomahawk, I knowed."

The lawyer folded his arms and smiled a little at the jury. "And who did that tomahawk belong to?"

Mr. Phelps turned and pointed at Indian John. "That Indian right over there. He always wore it stuck in a red sash around his waist. I seen it a hundred times if I seen it once."

I shook my head. Deciding who was telling the truth was like chasing a will-o'-the-wisp.

Augustus Root continued. "Anything else that you saw?"

"Well." The witness squinted. "We seen tracks in the snow all around the body. Lotsa tracks, like it weren't just one Indian who had set upon him with the tomahawk."

"Who did the tracks belong to? Did you know?"

The witness leaned back. "Yes, I did," he said slowly. "It weren't no trick to figure out whose tracks they was. There was three sets—two full-grown and one young. Since we knowed that the tomahawk belonged to him"—Mr. Phelps gestured toward Indian John again—"and since we knowed he always traveled with two other Indians, then we knowed 'zactly whose tracks they was. Weren't no trick to figure out Indian John was the one who kilt the trapper."

Mr. Phelps took a deep gulp of air and wiped his ragged sleeve across his face when he finished.

"No more questions." Augustus Root grinned and puffed out his chest.

Fool-headed old rooster.

"Mr. Kelley," the judge said. "Any questions?"

"Just two," Peter Kelley answered. He walked toward the witness, who shifted uncomfortably in his chair. "How deep was the snow?" he asked.

Mr. Phelps blinked. "Snow?"

"You said there was snow," Mr. Kelley repeated slowly, as if the witness was half-witted. "How deep was it?"

"Well now, I don't recollect things like that," Mr. Phelps stammered. "That was about three months ago. It was winter; we always got snow. Maybe it was six or eight inches deep. Maybe ten. Don't see what the snow has got to do with nothing."

Truth to speak, I couldn't see why Peter Kelley was asking about the snow either. Who could remember how deep the snow was on a particular day in March, and what did it matter?

"You said you saw tracks in the snow," Mr. Kelley continued. "Could you describe them for us, Mr. Phelps?"

The witness grinned widely. "I think most folks 'round here has seen moccasin tracks before, ain't they? Just picture a bunch of Indian tracks traipsed around in the snow."

"But I'm not sure I know what they look like," Mr. Kelley persisted. He frowned at the witness as if he

•151

was awful confused. "Could you describe what you saw for me?"

And suddenly, in a flash, I knew why he was being so curious about tracks and snow. *Snowshoes.* I cast a sideways look at Laura, and she gave me a half smile before turning away.

"You daft or what?" the witness said, shaking his head and setting the crowd to chuckling. He moved his hands in the air. "It's just a soft print like a foot, only without toes—like a footprint without toes." He smirked at Mr. Kelley. "Anything else 'bout Indians you want to know, Mr. Lawyer?"

"Just one more thing," Mr. Kelley said, rubbing the end of his nose. "Were you wearing your boots that morning you found the trapper? Do you recall?"

"Well, we warn't tiptoeing around barefoot, I can tell you that." Mr. Phelps rolled his eyes, and the crowd snickered.

"So if you were wearing boots . . ." Mr. Kelley paused as if he was putting all of the pieces together. "Why were the Indians wearing moccasins in the snow?"

"What?"

"I was just wondering why you saw moccasin prints, Mr. Phelps. Don't you think that the Indians would have been wearing snowshoes, like this one?" Mr. Kelley reached for something below his chair and then held up the exact snowshoe me and Laura had seen before. A strange silence fell over the room. "Don't Indians wear snowshoes in the winter months?" he kept on.

The air in the cabin was heavy and still. You could

tell folks were listening, even though they didn't like what they were hearing one bit. I figure most of the men must have known that Peter Kelley was right—that there should have been snowshoe prints, not moccasin ones, in the snow.

"I don't know—" Mr. Phelps stuttered and stumbled. A red flush crept up his neck, as if he was being slowly boiled inside. "I ain't sure, perhaps, I think maybe they was snowshoes, yes, I reckon they were."

"But you said you saw moccasin prints, didn't you? A footprint without toes?" Mr. Kelley repeated. "That's what you said."

The witness squirmed. "Now that I think—I'm sure they was snowshoes."

Mr. Kelley moved toward the witness chair. "Why don't you tell the jury the truth?" The lawyer's voice was low and angry. My heart pounded, fearing what would happen next.

"Tell them that you saw one set of snowshoes in the snow, Mr. Phelps." Mr. Kelley's voice rose. "One set of prints, not a whole band of Indians. One Indian—"

"I tol' you everything I know," the witness hollered.

The judge hammered his gavel sharply on the table. "You've had your try with this witness, Mr. Kelley. Return to your seat and leave well enough alone."

As Mr. Phelps got up, he shouted at the room, "Me and my family don't have nothing 'gainst Indians long as they stay in their place. And no matter what that Indian lawyer says, we done told you the gospel truth."

A lot of folks in the crowd clapped as the witness made his crooked, half-limping walk back to his seat. But I don't know why they clapped for him when they must have known, sure as I did, that he was outright lying. That he hadn't seen moccasin tracks, and maybe he hadn't seen any real tracks at all. Not a soul clapped for Peter Kelley sitting down, and it seemed to me he was the only one who was trying to find out the truth.

Up in front, Augustus Root called out in an easy voice, "Your Honor, my last witness is a trapper who was friends with the murdered man. He's setting outside waiting, if you'd like me to fetch him."

"Bring him in." The judge nodded.

But when the last witness walked into the cabin, dripping water from his hat, I know that my whole face must have turned as white as a cake of salt.

It was the same wretched, vulgar trapper who had once come to our door.

Twenty-six

"Why's he here?" I hissed to Laura, but she shook her head.

"Mr. Granger," Augustus Root said loudly after the trapper was sworn in. "Please tell us of your acquaintance with the dead man, if you would."

The trapper's eyes darted from one corner of the room to the other. He coughed a little and wiped his sleeve across his nose. "Me and the dead trapper Gibbs, we was good friends, that's what we was. Been hunting and trapping together for years," he added.

I squeezed my fingers together. I remembered the sixpence the trapper had tried to give to me. A sixpence to see the savage you got, he had said, and he hadn't breathed a word about the dead trapper being his friend.

Augustus Root kept on. "You weren't there the night he was killed?"

"Nossir. I was visiting a relation of mine."

"But you saw his body after Mr. Phelps found it?"

"Yessir." The trapper's eyes skipped over toward the jury. "It were an awful dreadful sight," he added slowly and loudly.

The lawyer looked closely at the trapper. "Didn't you find something near the body of your friend that day?"

My skin prickled.

Something near the body . . .

I remembered how the trapper had run from our house with something hidden in his hand. Something he had taken from us. Or from Indian John.

In the front of the room, the trapper reached into his coat. "This here is what I found." He coughed. "It was laying in the snow right next to the dead body of Gibbs."

Everyone stood up to see what he held. The floor creaked beneath the weight of boots and feet. Clambering onto the chest, I could see that the trapper held the same brown twist of paper I remembered.

Only it wasn't paper.

"You can tell for yourselves it came right from that savage's head," the trapper crowed. "Look at it."

It was a brown hawk's feather.

Twenty-seven

I wanted to holler that the miserable trapper had stolen the feather from this very cabin. That I had seen it in his hand when we ran him out the door. That he was telling nothing but lies.

But as I stood on the top of the chest and gazed over the heads of all of the people crowded into our house, I could see that folks believed every word the trapper was saying. A whole roomful of bonnets and hats nodded. How could I open my mouth to tell them what I had seen? What would my Pa do to me if I did?

My voice stuck fast in my throat and wouldn't confess a word.

"Sit down," Laura said, tugging on my hand. "Sit down, Reb. The judge is starting again."

"That trapper stole the feather from Indian John,"

I hissed as I clambered down from the chest. "It wasn't in the snow—I saw it in his hand when you ran him out the door. Somebody's got to tell the judge what the trapper's done—" My voice rose above a whisper, and Mrs. Hoadley turned to stare at us from the depths of her old green bonnet.

"You hush." Laura dug her fingers into my arm. "You just sit here and listen and keep quiet."

"Didn't you see that feather in his hand?"

"You want to face Pa and his wrath?"

"Did you see it?" I kept on.

Laura looked away. "No," she whispered. "Don't ask me again, no."

I ducked my head down as stinging tears rose up in my eyes. I didn't want Indian John to be kilt because of me, because I didn't breathe a word about the trapper's lies. If Indian John was kilt, maybe it would be my debt to pay in heaven. . . .

In the front, Peter Kelley stood up to ask Mr. Granger his questions. He gave the trapper a long, silent stare. It was so long that folks started to shift in their seats and whisper, "What's the matter with him?"

I started to hope that maybe Peter Kelley knew exactly what I did—that the trapper had stolen the brown feather. Perhaps Indian John had told him the story or he had guessed it for himself.

"You a God-fearing man, Mr. Granger?" Peter Kelley said to the trapper.

"Yessir, I am."

"You always tell the truth when you swear on the Bible?"

"Yessir, I do."

"Did you ever visit Indian John while he was a prisoner in this cabin?"

I drew in my breath and Laura gave me a fierce stare, warning me not to say a word.

"Nossir," the trapper answered.

I shook my head, and Laura pinched my arm. Hard. "Stop that," she warned.

Peter Kelley's voice was low and angry. "Are you certain?" He gestured toward the crowd. "I think there are a few people who might have seen you visiting here."

Laura gasped, and my face felt suddenly warm. Was Peter Kelley going to call on us?

The trapper shifted uncomfortably in his chair and glanced out at the crowd. "Come to think of it," he said, coughing, "it was a while ago, but maybe I did."

"So, you visited Indian John here?"

"Yessir, maybe so. But I don't recollect it real clear," he said, coughing harder.

"Did you take anything from him?"

"Nossir. Nothing."

"But if you visited here once, wouldn't it have been possible for you to take the feather from him then?" Mr. Kelley's voice rose. "And later say that you had found it near the body of your—"

Before the witness could answer, Augustus Root jumped up and hollered in his crackling old voice, "Stop this blasphemy, Your Honor!"

"Answer the question," the judge said tiredly.

The trapper set his shifting eyes on Mr. Kelley. "I already told you that the feather was in the snow. I ain't never seen it before or since, and I surely didn't take it from no savage's head."

Everyone was lying. It was nothing but lies.

"No more questions." Mr. Kelley finished, and my heart ached.

The judge pushed back his chair and stood up. Mr. Root's side of the case was over, he said, and after the noonday recess, Mr. Kelley would have his turn to call his witnesses. Some in the crowd hooted and laughed at the news.

"How many witnesses do you intend to call, Mr. Kelley?" the judge said.

"Just two, Your Honor," he answered. "Only two."

And the crowd hooted and laughed some more.

Twenty-eight

After folks left to eat their noonday meals, Mrs. Evans came over to talk to Laura and me. Settling herself on the edge of one of our beds, she rattled on and on about the evidence. "Ain't that lawyer Root something," she said in her never-ending voice. "That savage ain't got a prayer in the world, does he? Not with that tomahawk and that feather they found from his very own head."

I couldn't imagine how Peter Kelley would convince the jury otherwise. Not if they were all like Mrs. Evans, who only believed what was right there in front of her, what she could see with her own two eyes.

When the court resumed in the afternoon and Peter Kelley took his place at the front of the cabin, you could have heard the trees growing, it was so still. I think everyone was waiting to see who he would call to speak for his side and what evidence he would show. But I believe the crowd was downright startled when he stood up and called on Reverend Doan. What did he have to do with a murder trial?

Me and Laura watched as the small, frail man made his way to the front of our cabin, holding tightly to folks' shoulders as he passed. Reverend Doan had preached the sermon at Ma's funeral, and the cold March wind had turned his lips almost blue, I remembered.

"Good afternoon, Reverend Doan," Mr. Kelley said in a respectful voice after the minister was seated with the help of the sheriff. "You are a man of the cloth, correct?"

"I am." The minister nodded solemnly.

Peter Kelley held up the same plain hatchet he had shown earlier and asked the minister if black-smith Nichols had made it for him.

"He did." Reverend Doan nodded again. "Yes."

Some in the crowd mumbled that Reverend Doan was a half-witted old fool who wouldn't remember his own name if it was shown to him. Mr. Kelley didn't even give them a glance. He just studied a piece of paper in his hands until the room grew quiet again.

"I have only a few other questions for you, Reverend Doan," the lawyer continued after a long pause. "Even though I know you are a religious man, I was wondering whether or not you are inclined to gamble from time to time?"

"Gamble?" Reverend Doan answered, in a surprised voice. "Certainly not."

Some folks in the crowd snorted at the foolish question. They began to shuffle and move their feet impatiently, as if they figured Mr. Kelley was just pulling wool. Why in heaven's name was he asking such peculiar things? I wondered. What did gambling have to do with Indian John and the trial?

"Do you play cards?"

"No," Reverend Doan answered. "I do not."

Peter Kelley walked slowly across the room, gazing at the wood beams above his head. "But if one of your congregation members were to find a deck of cards in your coat—just imagine for a moment they did," he rambled on. "Would they be right, because of those cards they found, to accuse you of being a gambler?"

The reverend straightened his shoulders and thrust his old chin in the air. "Certainly not. I'm not a gambler and I don't play cards."

"But if they only believe exactly what the evidence shows, what is right in front of their eyes . . ." Mr. Kelley gave the jury a sideways look. Then if they found the deck of cards in your possession, wouldn't they think you were a—"

And suddenly I saw exactly what Peter Kelley was doing.

Augustus Root must have realized it, too, because he leaped out of his chair like a beech sprout on fire and hollered at the judge, "Stop this theatrical exhibition right this minute, Your Honor. This has nothing whatsoever to do with the Indian's trial. Nothing what-so-ever."

Augustus Root's little foot stomped furiously on

•163

the floor, and I grinned behind my hand. Laura ducked her head down and covered her mouth with her handkerchief, as if she was hiding a smile, too.

"Mr. Kelley," the judge said sternly. "Do you have any more questions for the minister that are pertinent to this case?" The way he pronounced the word "pertinent" made it sound as if it bristled with thorns.

Mr. Kelley shook his head.

The judge turned to Mr. Root. "You?"

"Absolutely none." Mr. Root glared.

The judge waved his arm. "The reverend is dismissed. You've made your point about the evidence, Mr. Kelley; proceed quickly with your last witness."

The audience leaned forward.

"My last witness," Peter Kelley said stubbornly, "is the Indian known as Indian John."

i am taken
to the talking chair and
my hand is placed on
the white man's spirit book.

the white man
speaks loudly
and holds my other hand
in the air,
but he does not
offer any tobacco
to the spirits
in the book.

i tell
the white chief
and his twelve strangers,
my name is Amik.
my people are Ojibbeways,
and my father is Chief Ajijaak.

my words are not
the songs of a bird,
i tell them.

my words
are the truth.

Twenty-nine

When they brought Indian John to the front of the room, he was followed by a man I had never seen before. A fur cap sat on the man's head like an odd-looking crown, and a long piece of silver dangled from his ear. Peter Kelley said the stranger's name was John Bigson and he would put Indian John's words into English.

Around me, people whispered that the interpreter was a half-breed savage, part Ottawa, and no one should believe a word either Indian said. Strange to say, Peter Kelley never mentioned that he understood Indian John's words himself. So I figured he didn't want the crowd to know he did.

While Indian John was being sworn in by the sheriff, Augustus Root raised an objection with the judge. He said that he didn't think Indians believed in the existence of God, so how could they be sworn to tell the truth on a Bible?

Peter Kelley answered sharply that Indians believed in their God as strongly as we believed in ours. I guess the judge must have taken Peter Kelley's side because he told Augustus Root that it was the truth that mattered, not the book. And if a Bible wasn't used, what book would Mr. Root suggest?

That made Mr. Root close his mouth fast and go back to his seat.

After Indian John answered the sheriff's questions, he was tied to the witness chair. I studied my checked apron. Tracing the pale edges of the apron squares with my finger, I tried not to look toward the front of the room. Someone had wiped the stripes from Indian John's face, perhaps it was Peter Kelley, and I was pleased to see that. But I didn't care to gawk and stare with the rest of the crowd.

After the sheriff finished, Peter Kelley walked to the front. From where I sat, I could see his shoulders rise up and then back down as he took a deep breath before he started.

"You have heard that the man who stands accused is called by the Indian name Amik." Peter Kelley waved his arm in the direction of Indian John. "His father is Chief Ajijaak. Amik has a wife and two children and travels with a small band of Ojibbeways— or Chippewas, as you call them."

I noticed that Peter Kelley's voice was full of nerves as he spoke. "It must be an awful hard thing to stand up there with his friend," I whispered to Laura.

"Amik has been accused of murdering the trapper George Gibbs in March of this year," the lawyer continued. "He has been held captive since the end of April inside this cabin, cruelly chained in the loft above our heads."

The crowd grumbled about the word "cruelly." I could see my Pa shaking his head at some of the other men sitting near the front.

Peter Kelley pushed on. "But, as you will hear, this Indian has never once harmed or murdered a white man. He is not guilty of breaking even the window glass of a white man's house. With his own words, he will describe for the jury what happened three months ago, in the month of March...."

And in a murmuring low voice, Indian John began to speak.

i tell
the white chief
and his twelve strangers
how Ten Claws, Se Mo, and i
set our traps
on the Old River of Many Fish
in the third moon—
the moon of crust on snow.

i tell them
the cold and bitter water
made our six hands slow,
but
we worked
and dreamed
of the soft fur pelts
that beaver and raccoon
would give to us
as they had
many times before.

i tell
the white chief
and his twelve strangers—
in two days' time
we returned to
the Old River of Many Fish
to check our traps.

•169

we walked forward and back,
forward and back,
looking,
and
we swept our hands
through the cold melting water,
searching,
and
we hunted for our snares
beneath the young trees.

but
all of our traps
were
gone.

Thirty

It was a curious feeling to hear the interpreter chang-ing Indian John's words into English, and to be told that the murmuring sounds that didn't seem to have any meaning at all were talking about ordinary sorts of things like catching beaver and raccoon for pelts.

Peter Kelley told the interpreter to ask Indian John what happened to the traps he set on the Old River of Many Fish. "Where do you think those traps went?" he told the man to say.

After the interpreter spoke, Indian John's eyes moved slowly across the crowd in a way that made everyone uncomfortable. If you have ever seen the way hunters study the woods, sweeping their eyes across every tree branch and inch of ground—that's the way Indian John looked at the crowded room.

People started to murmur that perhaps he was

casting evil spirits with his eyes. "Stop him from star-ing at us like that," one man hollered out. But then Indian John's eyes paused, and he raised his hand and pointed straight at someone in the crowd. I gasped. He was pointing at the miserable trapper called Granger.

*the trapper
who is in front of me,
and the one who is dead,
hunted where they had no right
to hunt,
i say.*

*they
followed our trail,
took up our traps,
stole the animals,
and placed their traps
on the Old River of Many Fish,
the river
that was
left to us by our ancestors
many strings of lives
ago.*

*i tell the white chief
and his twelve strangers—
we were angry,
angry
as the serpents
that thrash in the earth
below us.*

*but still
i did not raise up my hatchet*

against
the white men.

i tell them
it was Ten Claws
who was too much mad,
who crept out in the darkness
of night
and took his
tomahawk with him.
it was Ten Claws
who would not listen.

i tell them
i am a friend of Ten Claws,
and i am a friend
of the gichi-mookomaanag,
and i would not raise up
my hatchet
against one
or the other.

i did not kill
the white man.

Thirty-one

"That savage's nothin' but an outright liar!"

A big, pork-faced woman stood up and hollered so suddenly, I nearly jumped out of my skin. The judge had to pound his gavel for quiet, and he ordered the sheriff to take the woman out of the cabin. It took two men to pull her out by her elbows, shouting and hollering the whole time.

Once the room grew quiet again, Peter Kelley asked the interpreter to repeat what he said. I looked over at the jury men.

I couldn't tell what they thought of Indian John's story by the expression on their faces. Vinegar Bigger was cleaning his fingernails with a penknife, and the Hoadley brothers were slouched so far down in their chairs, they looked half asleep. Only Mr. Hawley seemed to be watching the proceedings with a careful

•175

eye. Did he believe what Indian John was saying? I wondered.

After the interpreter finished, some people in the crowd coughed loudly and shifted in their seats. An uneasy feeling had entered the cabin. It made me think of when Pa and the men played a game of cards—how the room would become suddenly tense and warm, and someone would get up to throw open a window or two.

In the front of the room, Peter Kelley folded the papers in his hand. "That was all I wanted the jury to hear, Your Honor," he said in a firm voice. "I wanted them to listen to Amik's own account of the events and consider carefully what he said."

Mr. Kelley's final, determined words seemed to stay in the air even after he sat down. I was real proud of him.

The judge nodded at Augustus Root.

With his hands clasped behind his back, Mr. Root took his time walking toward the witness chair, and he gazed rudely at Indian John for a few minutes. As if he was an exhibition that had come to town.

Sweeping his arm toward the jury, he said in a stinging voice to Indian John, "You expect the good hardworking gentlemen of this jury to believe you are a friend of the white man? A friend?" his voice mocked. "Yesterday you painted your face with the stripes of a savage, today you sit before us wearing the ornaments of a savage, speaking the language of a savage."

I could feel a lump rising fast in my throat, and I tried to brush away the angry tears that were filling up my eyes. My Pa put the stripes on Indian John's face. My own Pa.

But dreadful Mr. Root kept on.

"You expect the jury to believe that two white trappers trespassed on *your* river—what was it called?" Mr. Root looked at the paper in his hand. "Ah yes, the Old River of Many Fish." He grinned at the crowd. "You say the two trappers came to this river of yours, stole your worthless traps, took what you had caught, and that gave you the absolute right to put a tomahawk into the skull of one of them, am I right?"

Shaking sobs had begun to fill my whole chest, so I could hardly take a full breath.

In the front, Peter Kelley jumped up to object to the questions. "The defendant testified he did not kill the trapper, Your Honor," he hollered at the judge.

"Quite right." Mr. Root waved his papers in the air. "You're correct, Mr. Kelley. The savage testified that he sat in his tent all night in peace toward the white man while his Indian friend killed the trapper with a tomahawk."

I could hold back the tears no longer. As some of the men clapped and stomped their approval for Mr. Root, Laura whispered that if I couldn't keep hold of myself, I had best take Mercy and get outside before someone noticed me. Clinging to Mercy's little hand, I fled from the cabin.

Outside, it had stopped raining for a time. The pale green–leafed trees dripped water like wet wash on a line, and the gray clouds scudded across the sky. I took a deep, shuddering gulp of air, trying to forget the scene inside.

"You want to throw sticks?" I said to Mercy. "We'll go into the woods and throw sticks, how about that?"

For an hour or more, we hurled sticks at the trees. More often than not, Mercy's would fall only a few steps in front of her own feet, but mine would land hard and angry-sounding against the trees. Mercy laughed at the sight, and that made me feel some better.

By and by, Laura came out to find us. Standing on a dry patch of ground, she said the lawyers were giving their final speeches to conclude the trial and Peter Kelley had spoken real well. She told me she heard a few folks whispering that he had given a daring speech for as young as he was.

I wiped my hands on my apron. "Daring?"

"He told the jury that there were good Indians and bad Indians, the same as white people or any other people," Laura repeated. "And he said that the men in the jury were sworn to give Indian John as fair and full a trial as any white man. He told the men that no human life, not even an Indian's, ought ever to be taken away unless the accused was guilty of the crime. And the evidence proved without one shred of doubt that Indian John was as innocent as any one of them."

"You think the jury will believe him?" I asked, wanting to believe they surely would.

Laura was silent, looking out at the woods. "I don't know, Reb," she said uncertainly. "Perhaps after what he said, perhaps they might. It was a brave speech to give, it was. But I don't know."

The jury would meet and give their verdict the next day, Laura said. And then the whole terrible business of the trial would finally be done.

in the Ojibbeway game of
moccasin
you must watch
carefully
to guess
which moccasin
holds the marked musket ball.

you must look into the faces
of the moccasin players
and you must not be fooled
by their dancing arms or
their loud drum.
you must watch with your eyes
and guess what each one
is hiding.

when I look at the white chief
and his twelve strangers,
i think of the game
of moccasin.

Thirty-two

The jury deliberated inside Mr. Perry's store the next day. As the noonday hour crept closer, people began to gather outside the store, waiting to hear the outcome. More than a few of the men had brought their jugs of whiskey to toast the death of the Indian, they said. But I prayed hard that they were going to be proved wrong.

Me and Laura sat on a blanket in the shadow of the store, near Mr. Perry's woodpile. Mercy played with her yarn doll next to us. "He's innocent and the jury will see that, won't they?" I whispered to Laura for the hundredth time, and she said she hoped they would.

Mrs. Hawley came over and settled down next to us with her new little baby. "It's a trying day, isn't it?" Mrs. Hawley sighed. "Waiting for all the men." She smoothed her baby's straw-colored hair. He was a scrawny, squalling little thing.

Even in front of kindhearted Mrs. Hawley, me and Laura didn't dare to say what we thought about the trial. We just nodded politely and said it was a long wait, especially with all of the work left to be done.

Mrs. Hawley cast a look toward the store and shook her head. "I wish my husband wasn't even on that jury. He doesn't have any grudges against the Indians," she said softly. "It's the white man's word against the Indian's word, that's what my husband says—and who can decide which one to believe or what to do?"

I wondered if Mrs. Hawley's husband believed Indian John was innocent. Mr. Hawley was a quiet sort of man who seemed to do more thinking than most folks, so I hoped that he did.

Glancing over at Mercy, Mrs. Hawley turned her words in another direction. "Your little sister's growing up real fast, isn't she?" she said, and we agreed that she was.

When it was past noon, the doors of Mr. Perry's store finally opened. The whole crowd outside the store fell silent, seeing the jury men come out of the building one by one. I watched the men walk to a row of planks that had been set up for them as seats. The men didn't look to the right or left but kept their eyes to the ground. In the hushed silence, Mrs. Hawley's baby started screaming, and a trembling chill began inside me.

Judge James R. Noble and the sheriff followed the jury. The judge's black robes flapped around him like dark crow's wings. Close behind him came Augustus Root and Peter Kelley. At the sight of Peter Kelley's pale and drawn face, Laura's hand flew to cover her mouth and my throat tightened as if I would be sick. Mr. Kelley paused next to the judge's table with Augustus Root, and I could see his hands rolling and unrolling the brim of the hat he held. His face was the color of ashes.

One of the jury men walked over and gave the sheriff a piece of paper, and the sheriff carried it to the judge. I don't recollect what the sheriff said, but I won't ever forget what Judge Noble did afterward. He looked at the jury men and told them to pronounce their verdict to the crowd.

My heart hammered in my chest.

Each of the twelve men stood up one by one. The Hoadley brothers slouched and grinned as they said, guilty, guilty. Vinegar Bigger took off his old hat, pressed it to his chest, and mumbled, guilty. Shoemaker Nash said, "In my true and impartial judgment—guilty." Only Mr. Hawley paused a moment and looked out at the crowd before he said softly, "I believe he is guilty."

Peter Kelley's voice nearly broke as he jumped up right after Mr. Hawley and shouted, "Your Honor, the counsel, please, requests a new trial. The jury hasn't fairly considered—"

But Judge Noble shook his head. "The good men of this jury"—he glanced toward the men—"under tremendous responsibility have duly weighed all of the evidence. They have deliberated carefully and they have found the Indian called John Amik guilty of murder in the first degree—"

"But, Your Honor—" Peter Kelley's voice rose.

"Mr. Kelley—" the judge warned.

"The evidence was not—"

The judge leaned across his table. "Mr. Kelley," his voice thundered. "The verdict has been decided. The defendant is guilty. And the sentence will now be read."

As some of the men brought Indian John to stand in front of the judge, my ears throbbed and my head spun as if I would soon faint away.

The judge leaned forward, fixing his eyes on Indian John. "You, John Amik, have been found guilty of the crime of murder—do you understand that?" the judge said, and the interpreter, John Bigson, repeated the words. "The laws of God and man attach the penalty of death to the crime of murder."

Indian John did not move.

The judge continued. "You, John Amik, are no longer fit to live with the white man, and it is my duty to tell you that your time is fixed upon this earth. The court will allow you little more than a week's time to prepare for another world and to receive one visit from a representative of your people."

Standing up, the judge picked up a piece of paper and read in a loud voice, which echoed across the silent crowd. "It is therefore the sentence of this court that on the sixteenth day of June, about one week hence, between the hours of ten o'clock in the morning and noon, the Indian John Amik will be taken thence to the place of execution and hanged about the neck until he is dead."

And as the crowd stood and cheered around me and someone threw an egg at the front of Peter Kelley, I grabbed the cloth of my skirt in one hand, turned on my heels, and ran.

i do not understand
guilty
guilty
guilty
guilty.

i tell Red Hair
i have always stood in the smoke
between
our people.

i have not struck the gichi-mookomaanag
in their lodges
while they sleep.

and i have overlooked
the foolishness
of those
who would offend me.

to you, Red Hair,
i have been a protector,
a brother,

you will be sorry when
i leave you,
i say.

i tell Red Hair
i feel no fear
of death—
but i do not understand
guilty.

Thirty-three

It was Amos who found me.

I could have run off when I heard his stumbling footsteps coming through the brush and his voice calling out my name. But I didn't. The light was fading through the woods, and I sat at the foot of a big tree with my knees drawn up to my chin. My dress was covered with scraps of leaves, and my face was raw from crying. If Amos found me, that was his business. If he didn't, I would stay where I was and let the sun rise and set, rise and set, until I turned into a pile of bones and dust.

"There you is," Amos said in a peculiar voice when he turned his head and saw me. Walking over, he set his rifle on the ground and hunched down next to me. "Laura's worried sick."

I didn't answer. Just kept my forehead resting on my knees, not looking up.

Putting Laura's cloak over my shoulders, Amos sighed and sat down. "I know you feel softhearted about that Indian, Reb. Ever since you was toddling around the house, you always been that way. Never wanted to see us butcher the hogs or kill one of the calves. But it ain't gonna bring you any good to be that way, you understand what I mean? You've got to grow up and learn to see things different."

I didn't answer, just kept my head down.

Amos sighed again. I could hear him snapping little twigs between his fingers, one after another, as if he was thinking hard.

Without raising my head, I said, "He ain't guilty. I know he ain't guilty."

Amos kept on snapping twigs. In an even voice, he answered, "Don't be so foolish as to suppose that Indian John—or any other one—wouldn't put a tomahawk in your head or mine if they had half the chance."

"The witnesses lied," I kept on, my voice rising. "Every last one of them lied. Me and Laura know the truth." I didn't watch any of my words, just said whatever rolled off my tongue. I didn't care if I got in awful bad trouble with Pa. Or Amos either.

Amos sent a spit of tobacco at the ground. "Maybe they did lie and maybe they didn't. I don't know, Reb. But can't you see that it don't matter? Look at a wolf for instance—even if you knew a wolf had never kilt a sheep, would you let him stay in your sheep pen?"

"No," I said fiercely, turning my eyes on Amos. "But I wouldn't kill him neither."

Amos didn't answer, just snapped more twigs. Finally, he said, "What if seeing what happens to Indian John sends the rest of the Indians out of here for good and leaves us to live in peace? Wouldn't you rather live that way, Reb, instead of always fearing the Indians—always worrying whether or not you or Mercy were going to be carried off and kilt?"

"The Indians was on this land before us," I said, thinking of that arrowhead I found and Peter Kelley's stories of the Chippewas fishing on the river where he grew up.

"And that makes all this land theirs?" Amos stared hard at me. "That what you think, Reb? That we ought to give the Indians all this land that we cleared and planted and paid for?"

"I don't know," I answered stubbornly. "Perhaps."

"Get up," Amos said sharply. "I'm tired of your nonsense." He tossed his handful of sticks away and stood up. "Get up and brush yourself off, Rebecca, or I swear I will carry you back to the house over my shoulder. I don't want to say another word to you. Not one word."

Amos was as strong as an ox and he could have carried me all the way home like a sack of grain if he had a mind to. So, I didn't have no choice but to get up and follow him.

The woods were nearly dark as we tramped along the narrow, overgrown path. I could hear wolves howling in the distance, and Amos kept his gun at the ready, not saying a word. I followed a few steps behind him, and he kept turning and checking all the time to see that I was still there.

In my mind, I knew I could not stand by and watch as my wretched Pa and the other men hanged a man who wasn't guilty of anything except being an Indian. I would run off back to the East. I would go back to Ma's old family in Vermont.

Let them try to find me.

Ma always used to say, "It is better to suffer wrong than to do wrong." But it seemed to me that suffering a wrong, when you hadn't done anything wrong, was worse.

I couldn't forget the most awful sad look that crossed Peter Kelley's face as the verdict was read. And I wondered how Indian John must feel, being sentenced to die for a murder that he didn't carry out.

Perhaps it was better to do wrong than suffer wrong.

And right then, as I stumbled on a root in the dark woods, the smallest idea began to flicker inside me. What if I, Rebecca Ann Carver, did something terribly wrong to help someone who was innocent? The skin on my neck prickled at the thought.

What if I went against my Pa and Amos and all the men in the settlement who believed Indians were nothing but murderous savages? What if I freed Indian John before the hanging and let him escape?

I tugged the cloak tighter around my shoulders.

Perhaps that was what I would do.

in the darkness
of night
i sing and pray
to Kitche Manitou and the other spirits—
lead me to a good fire,
hear my cries, and
answer me.

a dream comes to me
while I sleep—
i hear the voice of the Thunder Beings
loud, loud, loud
as Midé drums.
i open my eyes
and see a cloud
black as a crow
circling, circling
above me.
in front of me
appears
a man
i have seen before
in spirit dreams.
he holds a palm
of tobacco
in his outstretched hand.

Amik, he says to me,
Amik,

why do you go about pitying yourself
when the wind,
the rushing wind,
will carry you
across the sky?

you must sing
to the Thunder Beings,
he says.
you must sing—
circle above me
a cloud,
circle above me
a cloud—
and the Thunder Beings,
they will come.

when I awaken
from my dream,
i know
what the spirit man says is true.
i know
i will not die.

Thirty-four

As I sat by the hearth the next morning, the question of whether to free Indian John spun around and around in my head. To defy my Pa and my settlement—and perhaps even the whole state of Ohio—seemed an act of madness. And what if I was caught? The punishment for setting a prisoner free was something I could not even bring myself to imagine. No one, not even Laura, would ever forgive me for doing such a thing.

I was so lost in my thoughts, I didn't even hear the soft knock on our cabin door. Laura was the one who called my name and waved her arm impatiently. Her hands were dripping wet from washing Mercy's mop of hair. "Go on," she said. "Reb, go on and answer the door."

Outside, I was struck speechless to see Peter Kelley

and an Indian woman waiting in our dooryard. The Indian woman was nearly as tall as Peter Kelley, and she stood to one side of him, leaving a wide space between them. Clusters of small tin cones dangled from her ears, and strings of colored necklaces hung from her neck like webs.

I stared at her as if she was a spirit come to life.

"I have brought Rice Bird, Amik's wife," Peter Kelley said in a voice that seemed close to tears. The woman's hands tightened on the white blanket she wore around her shoulders, but she did not look up. "Could we"—Peter Kelley's voice wavered—"come in for a moment to pay a visit to Amik?"

As they stepped into our house, Laura came forward, wiping her hands on her apron. "Rebecca and I are filled with sorrow and pity about what happened at the trial," she stammered. "Truly we are."

Peter Kelley didn't answer Laura at first. He looked down at his feet, as if he was thinking hard about something.

"I never believed the trial would end as it did," he said finally. "In the depths of my soul, I didn't. I thought that they would be fair, even with an Indian man. But I have learned something this week, Miss Carver." He glanced at Laura. "I have learned that all of the lawyers, and all of the courts, and all of the judges in the world will never change the hearts of men."

"Mine was changed," I said stubbornly.

Laura added that hers was, too.

But Peter Kelley just shook his head and didn't answer a word.

Turning to Rice Bird, he gestured at the steps to the loft, and she moved softly toward the stairway. It seemed that she didn't so much walk as float, like a lonely autumn leaf blowing across the floor, that's what she looked like to me.

Peter Kelley followed a few steps behind her. The hopeless way they appeared—the Indian woman by herself and Peter Kelley with his downcast shoulders—brought tears to my eyes.

As Rice Bird reached the loft, a dreadful sad wail began.

Me and Laura had to leave the cabin. We carried Mercy all the way to the springhouse and rolled a clay marble on a square of dirt, back and forth to her. Even from that distance, you could still hear the mournful, wailing cries of Rice Bird, and it was enough to break your own heart to listen to them.

my gentle Rice Bird
cries and weeps—
my love,
i do not wish you to go
on the road of the spirits—
i do not wish
to paint your face
or point your feet to the west
or place your medicine bag
beneath your head.

i tell Rice Bird—
Amik will not die,
not until
his children are old
and the line of his life is long
and straight.
you will see,
the Thunder Beings will save him.

Red Hair gives me a sorrowful look
as if i am a child
who cannot understand.
no, he says,
in a few days' time, Amik,
you will go to another place—
you will go to the land of the hereafter
and we shall never see you

on this earth
again.

i tell Rice Bird and Red Hair—
be not like two women.
bring me tobacco
for an offering
and build a nest for the Thunder Beings
near the place
where the gichi-mookomaan
prepares to end my life.

go away from me now, i say.
i have told you
what you must do.

Thirty-five

When Peter Kelley said goodbye to us that day, I knew we would never see the likes of him again. As Rice Bird waited at the edge of the woods, with her back turned toward us, he made his way to where we stood by the springhouse. Even little Mercy was still and silent, watching him.

"I wanted to tell you before I left that I was grateful," he said, trying to keep his voice steady. "For what you did. Even in spite of your own Pa. Even in spite of all the others. For showing some human decency and kindness"—he waved his arm in the direction of the house, and his voice broke—"to him."

Seemed like none of us knew what to answer. We looked away as Peter Kelley wiped his arm across his eyes.

Finally, Laura spoke. "Rebecca took him all the food and such. She's the most softhearted one."

"Bird Eyes," Peter Kelley said, looking up and smiling in the smallest way.

"What?" I replied.

Peter Kelley pointed at me. "Bird Eyes—for your quick, darting eyes." Then he turned to Laura. "Tall Girl Who Follows," he said. "That's what Amik calls each of you."

I had never thought of myself as being anything but plain and ordinary Rebecca Carver. Nothing worth noticing. To think that Indian John had given me a name when no one else called me anything much more than fool-headed and addle-brained made my insides ache. And how did he know that Laura was Tall Girl Who Follows? That she had been that way ever since Ma died. That she had stepped right into Ma's own footprints and left her own.

What had we given to Indian John? That's what my mind asked. I had left him foolish acorns and ribbons and paltry small things. When Pa wasn't watching, Laura had tried to give him extra helpings of our food. None of it amounted to very much.

"Isn't there something more that can be done?" Laura's voice rose. "With the judge or the laws, perhaps?"

Peter Kelley rubbed his eyes. "I would give away everything I have if I could save Amik. Everything I have," he said in a voice choked with tears. "Amik believes the thunder will save him. On the day of the hanging. The thunder," he cried, sweeping his arm toward the sky. "What could I tell him? I couldn't say that it wouldn't. I couldn't tell him that there isn't a thing that can be done for him. Not one thing to save him."

Peter Kelley put on his hat and turned away. "Thank you again," he whispered over his shoulder, and was gone.

If I was hoping that Peter Kelley would find a way to save Indian John, my hope was lost with him. As I watched his narrow shoulders and ill-fitting coat disappear into the woods, I had to brush the stinging tears out of my own eyes. I didn't dare to look over at Laura. She ran toward the cabin without a word, leaving Mercy and me behind.

Fine.

That's what I thought as I stood in the silence.

A thirteen-year-old girl without much courage or brains would go ahead by herself and find a way to free Indian John. Maybe the thunder couldn't save him, but I could. I would save the life of Amik, no matter what harm came to me.

That's what I decided.

Thirty-six

The idea for freeing Indian John came from a most unlikely place.

My brother Lorenzo.

A few days later, Lorenzo was sitting at the supper table, talking loudly with Cousin George and Amos. "You know what?" he was saying. "Me and Benjamin Evans climbed up and carved our names on that Indian's gallows yesterday morning."

I stopped my work near the hearth to listen.

"You know the gallows where they is going to hang the Indian, Amos?" Lorenzo kept on babbling. "That's right where me and Ben put our names. Right up there." He grinned. "All the boys is carving their names on the gallows. Never had a real Indian hanged here before, have we?" Lorenzo shoveled more pork and beans into his miserable mouth. "You gonna climb up there and carve your name, too, Amos, huh?"

"No." Amos shook his head while Lorenzo jabbered on.

"How 'bout you, George?"

George shrugged. "Don't know. Mebbe."

"You know that the hanging rope is already up there on the scaffold, George. It's three ropes twisted together, did you know that, George?" Lorenzo said. "So it won't break when he falls."

I caught my breath.

Break when he falls.

All this time, I had been trying to think of a way to free the irons that held Indian John in the loft. I didn't see how I could work them loose with my own small hands, not without a blacksmith, and even if I did manage to free Amik, I didn't know how he would ever escape from the loft without being seen.

Now a different sort of idea had come to me, though. What if I climbed onto the gallows and cut the rope to pieces? Or perhaps not cut it to pieces, but just enough for it to break when Indian John was hanged? Maybe he could escape into the woods surrounding the settlement and run. If I cut that big rope and folks weren't expecting him to fall, he might just get away before anyone realized what had been done.

But how could I slip onto the gallows without being seen?

From what Pa and the boys said, I guessed that the men had built the gallows on the open square next to Mr. Perry's store. But two taverns and

Nichols's blacksmith shop stood just on the other side of the street, a short ways down from the store.

So, if I climbed onto the gallows, I would be within eyesight of any soul passing down Water Street. A girl climbing a hanging scaffold in her dress and bonnet would surely catch everyone's attention. Unless—I stepped back so quickly from the hearth that I nearly knocked over Mercy, who was standing behind my skirts—unless the girl was dressed as a boy.

I looked closely at my brother as he kept on talking through his food. "That big rope would kill just about anybody, don't you think so, George?" he rattled on.

I wasn't much taller than Lorenzo or Benjamin Evans, and my legs and arms were just about as stick-thin. If I wore some of Lorenzo's clothes and one of his hats with my hair hidden underneath and climbed the gallows in the early morning, when everything was cast in shadows... perhaps no one would pay me any mind.

The rest of the evening, I rolled the idea over and over in my head. It was a plan with more things that could go wrong than right. But after several days of thinking, it was the only idea that I had.

Thirty-seven

On the last morning left before the day of the hanging, when it seemed almost impossible to wait any longer, I gathered up an armful of my brother's clothes and a sharp knife, and I crept from our cabin while everyone was still sleeping in their beds.

As I stood in the early morning darkness outside our cabin, I could not stop the awful shivering in my arms and legs. Surely I would never have the courage to climb the gallows when I reached it. That's what my mind said. And how would I cut the rope when I got there? How deep should I cut? And where?

A morning bird cried its lonely, sad sound somewhere in the shadows. It was as if that bird was worrying for me. As if it knew I ought not to try and save anybody.

I looked at the cabin door behind me and tried to

decide whether to turn back or go on. Laura was sleeping peacefully inside, and I knew I was causing her nothing but trouble by doing what I was, especially when she was trying her best to be a good Ma to me. And if Pa found out that I had sneaked away from her and tried to save the life of the Indian, both of us would be made to pay dearly.

But I couldn't keep away the thought of Amik either. If I turned back, he wouldn't have a soul in the world left to save him. I thought about the six little glass beads he had first given to us for the food we brought him . . . how he had named me Bird Eyes for my quick, darting eyes . . . how he hadn't done a thing that he was being accused of . . . how he was an innocent man who was being hanged because some folks had set their minds on hating Indians.

Standing there in the darkness, I remembered Peter Kelley's story of Old Turtle Woman. She had come all the way to his front door to save the life of his Ma. Even though she was an old Chippewa woman, she hadn't turned her back or let his Ma die. Telling my mind that I could be as brave as Old Turtle Woman, I took a deep breath and made up my mind. I started toward the settlement.

The Evanses' cabin was still dark when I passed it, and Vinegar Bigger's small place was, too. The only thing I could see was a thin wisp of smoke from his chimney. I stayed to the side of the narrow mud road, half running, half walking.

When I reached the edge of the settlement, I hid among the stand of trees behind Mr. Perry's store. I could see lights glowing in the tavern windows and one in the back window of Mr. Perry's store, where he lived. There were dark shadows of hogs moving and rooting along Water Street and a big horse tied up to a tree. But no people wandering yet. It was the time of the morning when the cows needed to be milked and fires tended, I told myself. No one would pay me any notice.

As I pulled on Lorenzo's worn trousers and his old linen shirt, I tried not to think about how I was destined to go straight to hell if any man caught sight of the shameful clothes I was wearing. Even Lorenzo's hat felt peculiar on my head with my hair piled inside it.

I had come this far, I told myself, and Providence had been with me. I had got out of the house and down the road without being seen, and I had pulled on my brother's trousers and shirt. All I had left to do was climb the gallows and cut the rope. The sun would be coming up fast. There wasn't time left to waste.

The gallows stood in the clearing next to Mr. Perry's store. As I moved out of the woods toward it, my heart trembled in my chest. A feeling of death seemed to drift around the gallows like a fog. You could almost see Death and touch it nearly. My mouth felt as dry as dust.

In front of me, the hanging platform rose from the ground like a pale wooden skeleton. Narrow steps went up one side. *Climb, Reb. Climb.* I kept my eyes fixed on the steps, counting them. My legs felt as heavy as millstones. There were nine steps—no, ten. They leaned some to the left.

Reaching the top, I could hardly bring myself to look at the place where the condemned man would be made to stand and the hanging beam that stretched overhead. The names of the boys were scratched fresh and scrawling all over the wood planks at my feet. *Lorenzo Carver. Benjamin Evans. Jacob Welsh. 1812.* The hanging rope lay curled in the corner of the platform, just as Lorenzo had said.

As I stood up there, my heart thumped in my chest and my face felt warm. It seemed as if I stood under a blazing pine torch and the whole world could suddenly see what I was doing. Pulling out the knife I carried, I could hardly keep my trembling fingers curled around it. It shook like a palsy in my hand. All I wanted to do was cut the rope as fast as I could and run.

A dog barked in the distance and I crouched down low and sawed the rope with a terrified fury. I put two cuts in it. They weren't very deep because I was frightened awful bad by the sound of the dog. Maybe I sawed through one of the three twists that formed the rope. I don't know. After I was done, I didn't even look at it. I just tore back down the steps and ran for my life.

Back in the woods, I couldn't recollect where I had left my dress and petticoats. I stumbled from tree to tree, trying to find them. The sun was slicing through the woods, and I didn't have time to waste. Pa and the boys and Laura would be awake and wondering what had become of me.

There. I saw the blue cloth of my dress. Snatching up the roll of clothes, I shook them and pulled them fast over my head. Stuffing Lorenzo's clothes and hat under my arm, I hastened through the woods. Seemed as if I couldn't take in enough air and I had a terrible sharp pain in my side.

As I drew nearer to our house, I heard voices.

My heart pounded. I didn't dare to be seen with the knife and my brother's clothes. Sticking them beneath a pile of leaves, I prayed a fervent prayer that when I returned to fetch them, a rattlesnake wouldn't be curled up in the middle of them.

When I came into the cabin clearing, my mean Pa stood in the dooryard.

I thought I would fall to pieces right then.

"Where the devil you been?" he hollered. "We been calling out for you."

I ran my tongue over my dry lips and tried to think. My heart thumped and thumped. "I took a basket of eggs over to the Hawleys, Pa, 'cause they ain't got none and I forgot to take them yesterday. They needed them for their breakfast. I didn't want them to have breakfast with no eggs. All their hens is dead."

Pa squinted his flint eyes at me, as if he could see right through all my lies.

I knew what he would ask next. Why had I taken the eggs so early in the morning? Before the sun was even up? And why had I left without telling no one? And where was my egg basket?

But instead, he cursed at the Hawleys. "All their hens is dead?" he hollered at me.

I dug my fingers into my palms, praying. "Yes sir, they is, that's what I heard."

Pa pointed his finger. "I don't want you giving no more of our eggs to them. You hear me, Rebecca?" he swore. "If they ain't smart enough to raise their own damn chickens, let 'em starve. We ain't their provider. Now git in here and help your poor sister with breakfast."

While we were fixing breakfast, Laura kept casting disapproving looks at me. "You best never do that again," she whispered, pinching my arm hard when no one was watching. "I was like to die when I saw you weren't in bed."

I told her I couldn't sleep, thinking about what would happen the next day, and so that's why I had decided to get up and take some eggs to the Hawleys for their breakfast. *God forgive me for lying to my kindhearted sister.* "I'm just awful sorry Pa found out about their hens," I added.

That part was true. Me and Laura had been giving eggs to Mrs. Hawley for more than a month.

It surprised me when Laura reached over and squeezed my shoulders, though. "I'm sorry, Reb, I don't mean to be cross with you," she whispered. "I know what a trying time this is. We'll just bear tomorrow the best that we can. It's the will of God, surely. You and me, we will bear it the best that we can."

My sister Laura had as much to bear as me, because Pa was sending her to the hanging to keep watch over Lorenzo, although she had pleaded and pleaded not to go. I was to be left at home with Mercy.

In my mind, I tried to picture how it would happen the next day. How Pa and the other men would climb the gallows, so proud of themselves for hanging a poor Indian. They wouldn't notice what had been done to the rope. The rope would break in front of their own eyes, and Indian John would be free.

But as the day wore on, I began to worry that perhaps I hadn't cut the rope deep enough. Or in the proper place. Or that Indian John wouldn't be able to get to his feet in time and run. That night, my mind tossed back and forth. I feared that there was something about the hanging that I had not considered. Something I had overlooked perhaps.

And as it turned out, I was right.

Thirty-eight

If I live to be a thousand years old, I will never forget what happened on the day of the hanging. How
the morning dawned warm and bright, as if the blue
sky didn't know an innocent Indian was going to be
hanged beneath it. And how Reverend Doan came
early to our house, before me and Laura had even
taken down the quilts strung between our beds.

I answered his soft knock at the door. Seeing old
Reverend Doan standing there with his Bible and his
black funeral clothes made the hollow feeling in my
stomach grow worse. "I have a small handful of tobacco to give to John Amik," he said in his frail voice.
"And I'd like to read the scriptures to him and pray
for his soul, if I might."

Pa, who was sitting at the table, told the minister
that he could read the Bible and give the Indian all

the tobacco in the wide world, but nothing would save an Indian's soul.

"All the same," Reverend Doan persisted, "I've come to try."

While the minister's thin voice droned above us in the loft, me and Laura cleared the breakfast table and tried to fix the clothes for Pa and the boys to wear. Laura was warming two of our flatirons in the fire so she could smooth the creases out of Pa's suit of clothes, and I was mending one of Lorenzo's shirts, when a rattling sound began outside our cabin. It sounded like the shivering noise of a rattlesnake's tail, only louder.

I turned to Laura. "What do you reckon that is?"

"What is?" She wiped her sleeve across her flushed, warm face.

"That noise."

"I don't hear a sound," she answered.

I moved over to the window to look out, and that's when I saw them.

Two crooked lines of men were marching out of our woods in a procession. Muskets rested on the men's shoulders, and they wore buttoned-up coats, even though the morning was already warm. There was a boy in front who I had never seen before, and he was keeping time on a drum.

My heart jumped with fear. What were they coming here for?

As the lines drew closer, I could see a few faces I knew among the strangers—Mr. Evans, and the Hoadley brothers, and William Grant, and Vinegar Bigger, who was wearing an old cocked hat with a feather—

"The militia's here," Lorenzo hollered, bursting through the cabin door.

"The what?" I whispered, turning away from the window.

Lorenzo waved his arm. "Come look at them, Reb. They're all gonna keep guard at the hanging of the Indian." He pointed at the door excitedly. "Pa told me there might be near fifty men from all over. I reckon that's how many there is, don't you think so, Reb?"

All my breath seemed to leave me at once. I didn't have words enough to answer Lorenzo. It took all the strength I had to keep myself from crumbling to the floor.

"Come and see the militia with me, Laura." Lorenzo turned and called out to my sister. "They're all dressed real handsome."

Shaking her head, my sister followed him outside. After the door closed, I couldn't hold back my tears. Rebecca Carver, my mind whispered, what a fool you are. You never counted on anybody guarding the gallows, did you? Never figured on the militia being called. Just thought you would be the one to save Amik.

What a fool you are.

i am placed on
the white man's wagon.
a flocking crowd
surrounds me.

i remember the story
of the old Ojibbeway man
who once saw the future as clear
as a reflection
in an unbroken pond.

the white spirits, said he,
will someday
number like sands on the shore,
and they
will sweep away
our people
from their sacred hunting grounds.

my heart trembles.
i gaze at the white spirits
moving and shifting
around me
like the sands on the shore
of a lake.

and I fear that the future
foreseen by the old man
has come.

Thirty-nine

Indian John was taken away in the Hoadleys' big wagon. I wish I had not turned back toward the window to see it.

When my Ma died, the minister told me to take one final look before the top of the coffin was nailed shut by Amos and Pa. Many times since, I had regretted seeing her lying in that coffin because it was the picture of her that always came first to my head. I could not forget how her face was the color of marble and turned a bit to the side, and how the piece of lace we pinned around her neck had come loose.

It was the same feeling with Indian John. He was led down from the loft by the sheriff, my Pa, and two other men. Reverend Doan followed them, still praying in his thin, wavering voice. I caught a glimpse of Indian John's soft moccasins moving past. There was one small flicker of color among the heavy leather boots, and then they were gone.

The Hoadleys' big plow horse stood in our dooryard, hitched to a wagon, and Indian John was seated on a pine box coffin in that wagon. His hands were tied behind him. In the bright light, the white blanket over his shoulder looked poor and unkempt.

I remember all of the people standing in crowds around the wagon. I stared at them, hardly able to believe how they gathered and grew like a swarm of sickening flies. There were women and children, even—with baskets of food and bed quilts for sitting upon. Poor Laura stood with Lorenzo, as Pa had ordered.

Angry choking sobs rose in my throat. Even in the darkest part of my mind, I couldn't understand how the whole settlement, and strangers, too, could come to gawk and stare at the hanging of a helpless Indian. How could they act as if an Indian's death, or anyone's death, was nothing but a fancy exhibition?

When the rattling drum began again and the wagon rolled forward, I could hardly see through the haze of tears and fury. Outside the window, the crowd of militiamen moved away in a blur of wool coats and muskets, and the women and children, wearing their Sunday best, trailed behind like a flock of mindless sheep.

As the last of the crowd disappeared from sight, I tore open the door of our house. "May the devil take all of you!" I shrieked at the empty place where they had been. "May the devil curse your wicked souls!"

And then I turned on my heels and ran in the op-posite direction with Mercy.

Clutching her hand, I ran toward my Pa's corn-fields like a person gone mad, filled with choking anger, intent on ruining everything I could lay my hands upon.

I would make my mean Pa and my brothers sorry for hanging a poor man who hadn't done a thing wrong. Stumbling from furrow to furrow, I be-gan to pull up the green growing blades of corn by the handful.

Pa said it was going to be a good year for corn, maybe the best ever. And a real good crop of beans and squash, too, everyone said. I ground my bare heels into the sprouts of beans and squash growing among the corn.

Mercy thought it was a game, and she followed me, tugging at the plants with her small fingers. But I ran on without paying her any mind, stumbling from one row to the next, trying to pull every bit of green out of the wretched brown earth that belonged to my Pa and brothers.

Let us go back east poor and hungry as paupers.

i stand
on the tall hanging place
of the gichi-mookomaanag.
the odor of death is all around me
and the sound of howling voices
roars in my ears.
my heart trembles
within me.

i twist my fingers around
the pinch of tobacco
in my hand.

Kitche Manitou, i whisper.
i do not want to die here
in a foreign place,
i do not want to die
among a people
who are not my own.
circle above me a cloud.
circle above me a cloud.

the gichi-mookomaanag
talk and talk.
they wag their fingers at me
and talk and talk.

i pray
to the spirits—

circle above me a cloud
circle above me a cloud.

the gichi-mookomaanag
talk and talk,
talk
and
talk,
they talk so much
they do not see
the clouds—
great piles of black clouds,
gathering
at the edge of the sky.

Forty

With all of my raving, I didn't notice the monstrous storm coming across the sky. I would have seen it, surely, if I had been watching. But my brain was turned, and so I saw nothing. I kept on tearing up blades of Pa's corn until my hands were cut and crossed with scratches, and the only sound I heard was a pounding, hammering fury inside my head.

I was in the middle of the field when the sky suddenly turned as dark as evening. It was as if someone had snuffed out the sun. The air became prickling cold, and an odd, wailing wind began to bend and toss the branches of the trees until you could hardly hear a word above the rushing noise. Pulling Mercy close to me, I looked up at the sky and gasped at the sight.

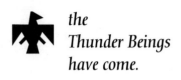 *the*
Thunder Beings
have come.

Forty-one

Rain and hail came down on our backs as if to pound us to pieces, and the claps of thunder shook the earth so hard I thought the world had surely come to an end. Me and Mercy lay in the field like two flat stones, and I prayed to God and Ma to save us. There wasn't a thing we could do, but lie in the mud and pray.

When the thunder finally moved off and the rain stopped, I didn't know at first if we were dead or alive. I wiped my eyes and lifted up my head. What I saw made me gasp. The cornfield was gone. Nothing but mud and water surrounded us, with bits of green scattered here and there like straggles of yarn.

Pa's corn was gone.

The weight of that sight took away all my breath. It was as if the storm had finished what I started with my own foolish hands. Only it had done far worse. I had just wanted to hurt my Pa and the boys. But the storm had taken away every growing thing.

Next to me, Mercy clung to my arm and cried to go home. "I'm scared, Reb, I'm scared," she wept over and over. "Take me back. Take me back." In her bedraggled clothes, she looked small and helpless, like a tiny bird. And for the first time in my whole life, I had the peculiar soft feeling of being a Ma. As if I was the Ma bird who was supposed to be look-ing out for her.

"Hush," I said, wiping the hair back from her face. "We're going on back to the house. Ain't nothing to worry about." Now, I hadn't carried Mercy since she was a toddling baby, but I picked her up after that and carried her all the way to the cabin with her tiny, wet arms holding tight to my neck.

The house was in a ruined state. When we got there, the fire on the hearth was out, and all the wood was soaked. Water had come down the sides of the chimney and run across the floor. Some of the shingles on the roof were gone, and one tree had toppled into the dooryard.

After all that had happened to us, I couldn't find the strength to move one foot more after we got back. I took off Mercy's clothes and wrapped her in a quilt, and then I sat in a chair by the cold hearth, not even bothering with my own rain-soaked dress.

Outside the house, everything seemed strangely silent. I thought about what Peter Kelley had said. How he waved his arm at the sky and told us Indian John believed the thunder would save him. Inside me, a terrible fear began to grow. A fear that perhaps the storm had swept away everyone in the settlement and spared only Mercy and me.

Heart pounding, I listened hard for the sound of Laura or the boys coming back. A hawk screeched above the trees. A wasp began to hum and peck at the window. And then, when the eerie silence seemed as if it would never end, I heard the sound of someone coming down the road. I jumped up.

"Rebecca!" a familiar voice called out. "Reb! Mercy! Are you there?"

It was Laura, running without her bonnet and as soaked to the bone as me.

When she reached where I stood in the dooryard, she pulled me tight against her big shoulder. "I was just so awful afraid of losing you and Mercy," she cried, her whole self shaking with sobs. "It just tore my heart to pieces, standing inside that store knowing you and Mercy were by yourselves in the storm. I didn't know what I'd find when I got here. I didn't know what terrible sight I'd find."

It was hard to keep my voice steady to tell her that me and Mercy were fine. We had been caught in the storm, I said, but we were both fine.

Laura wiped her eyes and glanced at the cabin. "And Mercy's inside?"

I nodded.

The question I wanted to ask, and didn't want to ask, seemed to hang in the air between us. I didn't want to grieve Laura more by asking it, and I think perhaps she didn't want to cause me grief by answering it. So, neither one of us spoke. We just stood there in the dooryard for a long while, taking account of all that the storm had done around us.

But the question would not keep silent.

"I want to know—" I hesitated and my voice stuck in my throat. I looked up at the sky and took a deep breath. "I want to know what happened to Indian John."

"Reb," Laura began. "I don't—"

I pressed my lips together stubbornly. "I want to know."

Laura sighed and gave me a sorrowful look. "I'll tell you what I saw," she said finally, shaking her head. "May God forgive me, but I'll tell you what I saw."

Laura said that Indian John was taken to the gallows near Mr. Perry's store. Some of the men who brought him there gave speeches, and then the reverend offered a short sermon and two prayers. "He spoke some kind things about the Indians, Reb," she said. "Real kind things."

All the while, Indian John stood on the gallows with the hanging rope around his neck. It was nearly an hour, she told me, before the order for execution was given.

"I had to look away, my stomach was so sick, Reb." Laura's voice shook. "How could they do that to a poor man? How could they?"

I swallowed hard.

"His body crumpled to the ground, Reb," Laura said, closing her eyes. "The hanging rope broke above him—"

My eyes flashed toward Laura. "The rope broke?"

"I turned and saw his body on the ground as the storm fell upon our heads," Laura answered quietly. "May God save the poor man's soul. That's what I prayed as we ran for the shelter of Mr. Perry's store. The whole crowd ran. I thought we would all be swept away in the storm. I had hold of Lorenzo's hand in the scattering crowd and we ran toward the store, with the wind and thunder roaring around us as I have never heard before in all my life."

I was silent, picking at the cloth of my skirt with my fingers.

"So, he is dead," I said softly. "They have buried his body, and he is dead."

"No," Laura answered in a trembling voice. "That is what has unsettled everyone, all of us who were there." Laura turned and stared at me. "I saw his body on the ground with my own eyes, Rebecca, truly I did. And Pa said when the storm hit, he lifted the body into the coffin with the help of the sheriff and four other men. And Dr. Weston said that all life had expired. But when the storm ended and the men re-turned to the gallows, the body was missing from that coffin, and no one knows where it has gone."

No one knows where it has gone.

i am
a running deer
i am
a soaring bird
i am
a diving fish
i am
a rippling snake
woods
sky
water
day night
night day
i run

Forty-two

Inside my mind, I wanted to believe that Indian John had escaped from the hanging. I told myself that perhaps by cutting the rope, I had saved his life. That maybe he had lifted up the cover of that coffin, in the middle of the storm, and run off into the woods. I knew it was an impossible thing to believe, but I did.

My Pa and brothers figured that the body had been stolen by some of the strangers who had come to the hanging. When he got back from the settlement that evening, Pa raged on and on about it. "I know it was some of them men from up near the mills. I heard them talking about how much that body would fetch if they had it. They went out in that storm and stole it while we was inside Perry's store, I swear they did," he hollered at Amos and George. "I'll go and hunt them down myself, I swear I will."

Me and Laura didn't breathe a word the whole time Pa was hollering. We just kept our eyes on our work, and Mercy slept through it all in our bed.

Pa and the men left for the mills real early the next day. They took the empty coffin with them in Mr. Hoadley's wagon. We watched them roll down the road—about fifteen men in the wagon with their rifles—and I prayed hard that they wouldn't come back with Indian John's body.

While they were gone, me and Laura put the house in order and set the rain-soaked clothes out in the warm sun. Pa didn't tell us to straighten up the loft, but me and Laura went up there first and swept the whole dusty floor, even the farthest corners. I figure both of us were trying to erase all that had been there.

While she was moving the straw bed pallet, Laura found the little gifts I had once given to Indian John. In the dim light of the loft, they suddenly scattered across the floor. An acorn. A bird nest. A scrap of green ribbon. A brown butterfly wing. I caught my breath, waiting for Laura to say something.

But I think she must have guessed exactly where they had come from, because she picked them up without a word and gave them to me. Although I feared she would give me a scolding, she never did ask me another word about them.

Pa and the boys returned after dark without finding a trace of the body. Amos told Laura that some of the men were starting to wonder whether or not Indians had stolen the body and buried it, and a few, like old Vinegar Bigger, even thought the terrible storm was caused by them, too.

Pa said that Vinegar Bigger's kind of thinking was pure nonsense. If the Indians had power over the heavens, Pa said, they would have sent droughts and windstorms and floods and run the white man off the land long ago. And furthermore, even if the Indians had caused the storm to come, it hadn't done Indian John a bit of good, had it? They had still hanged him, and he was gone forever and dead.

No, my mind hollered at my Pa. He ain't gone forever. Or dead.

But five months would pass before we would find out the truth about Indian John. And the truth would come from an unlikely person—old Reverend Doan.

Forty-three

November 1812

Me and Laura were putting up provisions for the winter on the morning that old Reverend Doan came to our door. It was early November, and most of the men were still away. Pa and Cousin George had left in late summer to fight in the war that had started against the British and the Indians.

Sometimes it was hard to keep count of all that had happened since the trial and hanging of Indian John: the storm that ruined most of the young corn; the news of the war with the British reaching our set‑tlement at the end of June; even Laura finding her first beau. A young schoolmaster named Mr. Josiah Elliott had arrived in our settlement in August when nearly everyone else seemed to be leaving on account of the war.

Laura Elliott, now that would be a fine name, I liked to tell her.

We were in the middle of our work when Reverend Doan came to call on us. I remember how I opened the door to find him standing there. His thin face was pinched and red from the November cold. "Might I come in?" he said.

Although we couldn't imagine why he had come to visit when no one was sickly or in need of his prayers, me and Laura invited him inside to warm himself with a cup of tea. He took a long while to drink it, and I feared he would surely drop our good teacup with his trembling hands.

But after a long silence, he said in his frail voice, "I was asked to bring a message to you when I passed through the settlement again. The lawyer Mr. Kelley told me you would know how to take it to a young girl known as Bird Eyes and her sister Tall Girl." Reverend Doan gazed at us in a peculiar way. "Have you heard of them?"

I think me and Laura were both too stricken to say a word, but the reverend didn't seem to notice. He continued on, without waiting for us to answer.

"You are to tell them that their friend has not died as everyone believed, but he has gone away with his family and still lives. Gone away and still lives." I hardly dared to breathe as Reverend Doan rattled his empty teacup onto the saucer and looked at us. "Can I trust you to give this message to those for whom it is intended? You'll remember everything exactly as I've said?" Me and Laura just nodded.

"Fine, then." He stood up slowly and put on his old hat. "God rest your dear Ma's soul," he said as he left.

Indian John had lived.

In my mind, I tried to picture Amik and Rice Bird and their little band of Chippewas slipping away to another place—far away from Ohio, far away from the Crooked River, far away from the growing war.

But even then, I think we also realized that they would never be able to return. That they would be the last Indians any of us ever saw on the Crooked River. So, the word of their escape made us feel both sweet and bitter at the same time. Like the trees in springtime, sweetness and bitterness both.

when i finish
my story,
the fire-blaze is low.
the eyes of the Little Ones—
children of children—
grow heavy with sleep.

you must not forget
the story of your grandfather,
i finish softly,
you must tell it
to your children
one day when you are old
and to your children's children
for many
strings of lives to come.

Rice Bird shakes her head
and clucks her tongue at me.
it is late,
old talking grandfather,
come to bed.
it is late. they are asleep.
come to bed.

but i do not listen.

outside
the sounds

of the land that is not ours
grow quiet.
the sounds of the people who are not ours
grow silent.

i sit by the soft fire,
circle my lips around
my old tobacco pipe,
and remember
when we were not
a poor people,
when the trees did not
weep for us.

i remember Ten Claws and
Small Hawk and my father Ajijaak,
and the others
who are gone
on the road to the spirits.

i remember the young girl
who left gifts
of acorns and bird nests
at my feet.
and i remember Red Hair, my old friend.

when i close my eyes,
i see the Crooked River and
the rolling forestland

where we hunted
and fished
and dove like arrows
long
ago.

i am old now, i whisper,
but i still remember.

About Crooked River

What is the truth—*débwewin*—and what is the fiction in the story of John Amik? Although *Crooked River* is a work of fiction, the idea for this novel began with an actual trial. In 1812, a Chippewa Indian named John O'Mic was held captive for two months, tried by a white jury, and convicted of murder in Cleveland, Ohio.

As I delved deeper into this story, I learned that the year 1812 was a time of particular unrest and growing fear in this region—among both whites and Native Americans. One historian wrote, "Nowhere on the American frontier was the clash of cultures more violent than on the Ohio frontier."

During this turbulent period, the legendary Shawnee leader Tecumseh was trying to create a confederacy of Indian nations from Alabama to the

Northeast to negotiate for Indian lands and protect them from further loss to white settlement. War between Great Britain and the United States loomed on the horizon, and the British were supplying weapons to Indian nations. At the same time, white settlers continued to push westward—often breaking agreements made in earlier treaties with the Indians. So, as I researched this story, I began to see that the imprisonment and trial of John O'Mic took place in an environment of growing conflict and violence.

I was also surprised to learn that John O'Mic was held captive in the cabin of a settler who had his family living inside the cabin at the same time. His family included a small child, a thirteen-year-old girl, and a young woman. What did they think about the Indian imprisoned in the loft above them? I wondered.

When I write about history, I am often interested in the side of the story that has not been told. So, I began to consider writing about the events of 1812 from the perspective of one of the children in the cabin. At the same time, I found myself drawn to the voice of John O'Mic. What was *his* story? What would he say about the events as they unfolded around him? That is how *Crooked River* became a "two voices" story.

The language of the Carvers came from books, letters, and journals of this time period. Phrases such as "truth to speak," "white as a wall," "strange to say," and "worn to shadows" came from these places. An important source for Rebecca Carver's voice was the unpublished diary of a young girl named Emily Nash, who lived in northern Ohio during this time. In fact, Peter Kelley's rattlesnake story was based on a dramatic account in her diary.

Sadly, the language of the past sometimes reflected the prejudices and hatreds of the past. Some of the characters in *Crooked River* use words such as "savages," "half-breeds," and "beasts" to describe the Native American people. It was with a heavy heart that I put these words into the story. They were used on the frontier and found in the historical documents I read. Appallingly, even the governor of Ohio used this language in an 1812 address to the Ohio legislature in which he called the Indians "hordes of barbarians." As a historical writer, I could not ignore the language of the past, but I hope that it causes readers to reflect upon the destructive nature of these words.

Although the word "Indian" was used in the past, many Native Americans feel it is a word that does not accurately reflect the diversity and history of their cultures. "Native American," "First Nations People," and "indigenous people" are more frequently used today.

While I have used the common name "Chippewa" for this novel, I should point out that the Chippewa nation is known by several different names. The ancient name for the Chippewa people is the Anishinabek, which translates as "original people" or "beings with bones, flesh, and spirit."

In the 1800s, "Chippewa" was the name that white people often used for this nation. During this time period, the people of this nation usually called themselves the Ojibways. The name can also be spelled "Ojibwe," "Ojibwa," and "Ojibbeway."

As I studied the language of the Ojibwe people, I was fascinated by the beauty of the words and their sounds. Ojibwe is sometimes called a verb–based language because of its emphasis on words that describe action and movement. I chose to use story-poems for John Amik's voice because I felt that poetry best reflected the powerful, descriptive language found in the speeches, songs, and stories of the Ojibwe. A wonderful resource for exploring the poetry within Native American songs is *I, the Song: Classical Poetry of Native North America,* edited by A. L. Soens.

Whenever possible, I used Ojibwe words and phrases in John Amik's passages. Phrases such as "many strings of lives ago," "when the trees did not weep for us," and "his words roll like logs in white water" all come from Ojibwe sources. Since dreams hold great spiritual power for the Ojibwe people, I wove together dream descriptions from several Ojibwe songs and stories to create Amik's spirit dream.

During the research and writing of *Crooked River,* the most memorable moment for me occurred when I read about *Animiki*—the Thunder Beings, or thunderbirds—who are a powerful element of the spirit world for the Ojibwe people. I was fascinated to discover that there are a number of stories and songs within the Ojibwe oral tradition that tell of captives or others being saved by the powerful Thunder Beings. The chant recited by John Amik, "circle above me a cloud," comes from one of those songs. The image at the top of Amik's chapters is a thunderbird.

In the Cleveland trial of John O'Mic, a storm did suddenly appear at the moment of his execution. White observers called it a "terrific storm which came up with great rapidity" and described how the crowd scattered in its wake. So, *Crooked River* gave me the opportunity to weave together written history and oral history in a unique way.

Although most of the details of John Amik's trial have been imagined, I used accounts from several Indian trials in Ohio and elsewhere to create the fictional trial scenes. A trial in 1821 involving the testimony of a well-known Seneca leader named Red Jacket provided the scene where the use of the Bible is questioned, for instance. The place names found in the novel are also fictionalized for the most part; however, the name "Crooked River" has sometimes been used to describe the winding Cuyahoga River near Cleveland, Ohio.

Although the homeland of the Ojibwe nation once stretched throughout the Great Lakes region, only small areas of land still remain. For decades treaties were made and broken by the United States and the government agents who negotiated them. Today, reservation lands exist in Minnesota, Wisconsin, Michigan, and the Dakotas as well as Canada. However, there are currently no lands in Ohio that are held by the Ojibwe people or any other Native American nation.

While working on this novel, I often drove on a road called Chippewa Road, past a housing complex called Chippewa Place, over a river called Chippewa Creek. The story of John O'Mic caused me to stop and wonder, What do these names mean? Who were—and *are*—the Chippewa people? When were they here? Why did they leave?

Crooked River gave me a glimpse into the lives of the frontier people and the "original people," the Chippewa. Although I am not of Chippewa heritage, I believe that all of us, of any background or culture, can *begin* to understand one another and the places of our present and past. There is still much more to be learned, but I am honored to have been given the chance to try.

—*Shelley Pearsall*

Selected Bibliography

Baraga, Frederic. *A Dictionary of the Ojibway Language.* St. Paul: Minnesota Historical Society Press, 1992.

Bial, Raymond. *The Ojibwe.* New York: Benchmark Books, 2000.

Bourgeois, Arthur P., ed. *Ojibwa Narratives of Charles and Charlotte Kawbawgam and Jacques LePique, 1893–1895.* Detroit: Wayne State University Press, 1994.

Densmore, Frances. *Chippewa Customs.* St. Paul: Minnesota Historical Society Press, 1979.

Hurt, R. Douglas. *The Ohio Frontier: Crucible of the Old Northwest, 1720–1830.* Bloomington: Indiana University Press, 1996.

•245

Jefferson, Thomas. "Letter to Benjamin Hawkins, August 13, 1786, Paris." Library of Congress, Thomas Jefferson Papers Series 1, General Correspondence, 1651–1827.

Johnston, Basil. *Ojibway Heritage.* Lincoln: University of Nebraska Press, 1990.

Kirkland, Caroline M. *A New Home, Who'll Follow?* Edited by Sandra A. Zagarell. Piscataway, N.J.: Rutgers University Press, 1990.

Nelson, Larry L., ed. *A History of Jonathan Alder: His Captivity and Life with the Indians.* Akron, Ohio: University of Akron Press, 2002.

Nichols, John D., and Earl Nyholm. *A Concise Dictionary of Minnesota Ojibwe.* Minneapolis: University of Minnesota Press, 1995.

Soens, A. L., ed. *I, the Song: Classical Poetry of Native North America.* Salt Lake City: University of Utah Press, 1999.

Stone, William L. *The Life and Times of Red Jacket.* New York: Wiley and Putnam, 1841.

Tanner, John. *The Falcon: A Narrative of the Captivity and Adventures of John Tanner.* New York: Penguin, 1994.

Van Tassel, David D., and John J. Grabowski, eds. *The Encyclopedia of Cleveland History.* 2nd ed. Bloomington: Indiana University Press, 1996.

Vennum, Thomas, Jr. *Ojibway Music from Minnesota: A Century of Song for Voice and Drum.* St. Paul: Minnesota Historical Society Press, 1989.

Warren, William W. *History of the Ojibway People.* St. Paul: Minnesota Historical Society Press, 1984.

MUSEUM RESOURCES

Van Andel Museum Center
Public Museum of Grand Rapids
Anishinabek: The People of This Place (permanent exhibit)
272 Pearl Street NW, Grand Rapids, MI 49504

Ziibiwing Center of Anishinabe Culture and Lifeways
Saginaw Chippewa Indian Tribe of Michigan
6650 East Broadway, Mount Pleasant, MI 48858

Acknowledgments

I would like to gratefully acknowledge my editor, Joan Slattery, assistant editor Jamie Weiss, and my agent, Steven Malk, for their guidance and encouragement. My gratitude to Marcy Lindberg for her continuing support. I am also indebted to Dr. Philip Weeks, Professor of History at Kent State University, Matt Lautzenheiser and Karen Lohman of Hale Farm and Village, and Jackie Fink, who reviewed early drafts of *Crooked River*.

Finally, a special thank-you to the following young readers, who took the time to read and share their thoughts about the manuscript: Virginia Angelo, Samantha Ballash, Alex Bruck, Karilynn Cotone, Alex Coundourides, Mandy Czaplicki, Ashley Erlanson, Dominick Ferlito, Lauren Fiffick, Leanna Gruhn, Rebecca Hannan, Crystal Hill, Tim Hogan, Jack

Holzheimer, Matthew Marecki, Mariana Medakovic, Shauna Nighswander, Jackie Piatak, Van Pollard, Sarah Popovitz, Vicky Reynolds, Josh Rikard, Emily Rosko, Lauren Saintz, Zach Scicchitano, Christine Smienski, Dan Sweet, Matt Unger, Bridget VanDen-Haute, and Molly Vogel.
Miigwech.
Thank you.

Shelley Pearsall is the author of the acclaimed *Trouble Don't Last*, winner of the Scott O'Dell Award for Historical Fiction. A former teacher and museum historian, Shelley Pearsall now writes full-time from her home in Ohio. To learn more about the author and her books, please visit www.shelleypearsall.com.